Lamplighter

**Other Books by
Bernice Thurman Hunter**

Amy's Promise

Janey's Choice

Booky: A Trilogy

> *That Scatterbrain Booky*
>
> *With Love from Booky*
>
> *As Ever, Booky*

Hawk and Stretch

A Place for Margaret

Margaret in the Middle

Margaret on Her Way

The Railroader

The Firefighter

Bernice Thurman Hunter

Lamplighter

Cover by
Tony Meers

Scholastic Canada Ltd.

Scholastic Canada Ltd.
175 Hillmount Road, Markham, Ontario L6C 1Z7

Scholastic Inc.
555 Broadway, New York, NY 10012, USA

Scholastic Australia Pty Limited
PO Box 579, Gosford, NSW 2250, Australia

Scholastic New Zealand Limited
Private Bag 94407, Greenmount, Auckland, New Zealand

Scholastic Ltd.
Villiers House, Clarendon Avenue, Leamington Spa,
Warwickshire CV32 5PR, UK

Canadian Cataloguing in Publication Data

Hunter, Bernice Thurman
      Lamplighter
ISBN 0-590-71373-6
I. Title
PS8565.U577L3 1987   jC813'.54 C87-094769-9
PZ7.H86LA 1987

11 10   9   8 7   Printed and bound in Canada   9/9 0 1 2 3/0

For my sister, Wilma, and brothers,
Gord, Jack, and Bobby

Contents

Chapter 1
Early to rise

The loghouse was pitch dark when little Willie woke. At first he could not imagine what had wakened him. Then he heard the muffled voices of his parents drifting up from the kitchen below. He strained his ears towards the bare pine floor but could not make out what they were saying.

There was no moon that hot July night in the year 1888 and no stars shone through the chinking in the squared-log walls. Willie was not allowed to light his own candle so he lay staring into the darkness.

His brother, Artie, slept soundly beside him on the cornhusk mattress. The dried cornhusks made a terrible noise if you moved about, so Willie lay still, afraid of waking his big brother. Artie was ten, and Willie was only six-and-three-quarters, and Artie had a bad temper, so Willie lay still.

He needed to use the chamber pot under the bed but he didn't dare. Then his nose began to itch and he was scared to scratch it. Finally, when he could stand it no longer, he inched his fingers up the patchwork quilt. The mattress went crackle, crackle, crackle and Artie stirred and mumbled. Willie sighed and tried to relieve the itch by wriggling his nose.

He could hear old Grandpa snoring in the next bedchamber. Then old Grandma must have pinched his nose together because there was a sudden loud snort, then silence.

His sisters, Nellie, Alice and May, slept side by side on the straw mattress in the bedchamber at the head of the stairwell. The straw mattress rustled, too, but not nearly as loudly as the one stuffed with cornhusks.

When I grow up and be a man, vowed Willie to himself, I'm going to have me a real feather tick like Mama says Uncle James has in his house.

The feather tick got him to thinking about Uncle James. He was Mama's youngest brother who came up north twice yearly to visit them. Willie always looked forward to seeing him, but there was one thing that vexed him about Uncle James's visits. Every time he came he asked his nieces and nephews the same question: "What are you going to be when you grow up?"

Willie had no notion what he was going to be. Artie said he would go out west and be a rancher. Nellie wanted to get married and be a mother. May planned on being a schoolmistress. And Alice's ambition was to be a nurse in a big city hospital. Willie knew that Alice's answer pleased his mother best of all because it was she, Emily Adams, who nursed the sick, comforted the dying, and helped new babies be born in their little northern community.

But Willie never knew what to say, and Uncle James's question made him hang his head and feel foolish and ashamed.

Suddenly his thoughts were interrupted by a flickering light in the hallway. He heard the creak of the worn wooden steps and the swish of his mother's long skirts. Then her face appeared in the doorway, softly lit by the warm glow of a candle.

"Willie! Get up quiet and come down, there's a good lad."

He obediently eased himself out of bed and the cornhusks crinched and crackled. Artie grunted and turned over. Willie tiptoed quickly after his mother down the dark staircase.

The stairwell was in the centre of the loghouse. Upstairs it led to the four small bedchambers. Downstairs it divided the house in two. On one side was the seldom-used parlour, on the other side the much-used kitchen.

Closing the stairwell door silently behind them, his mother blew out the candle. They didn't need its tiny light now because the big oil lamp burned brightly on the rough-hewn table. In its light Willie could see Papa seated at the table eating his breakfast.

In spite of the heat of the summer's night, a brisk fire burned in the cookstove. At the back of the stove a black iron kettle gave off little puffs of steam.

The grandfather clock tick-tocked in the corner. It said ten after four in the morning. (Willie was glad May had taught him how to tell the time.) He wondered what was happening, but he didn't dare to ask. He had been well taught by a strict father that children should be seen and not heard.

Samantha, the housecat, came out from under the hot stove yawning and stretching. Noiselessly she brushed past Willie's leg.

"Good morning, Sam," whispered Willie, letting her long grey tail slide smoothly through his fingers.

"Meow!" she answered, then began to sharpen her claws on the old pine table leg.

"Scat!" hissed Papa threateningly.

Willie's heart went thump. It wouldn't be the first time that Sam had felt the toe of Papa's boot.

"Good gracious me!" declared Mama, flapping her apron to shoo the cat away. "She'll have that poor old table leg worn to a sliver in no time at all so she will."

"Why does she always pick the same table leg to scratch on, Mama?"

"Cats be strange creatures of habit, Willie."

Willie stroked Sam's head and she began to purr. He liked Sam, but he would have liked her even more if she wasn't so clever at catching mice. He was ever so fond of the tiny field mice with their shiny eyes and pointy ears. And he hated to see them hanging limp and lifeless from Sam's mouth. Yet he knew it wasn't her fault. It was her duty to keep the loghouse free from vermin. It was how she earned her keep.

"Wash up, Willie," whispered his mother.

The washbasin stood on a wooden bench, the soft-soap tin beside it. Under it were two buckets of water. One was rainwater, the other fresh water from the spring.

With the long-handled graniteware dipper that hooked on the side of the pail, Willie half-filled the basin with amber-coloured rainwater. Then he chose a scrap of soap from the tin. The yellow soap made by his mother from hardwood ash and the velvety soft water gave a lovely foamy lather.

"Scrub behind thine ears," reminded Mama.

He did. Then he reached for the drying flannel

that hung on a wooden peg attached to the window frame.

Meanwhile his mother had filled his bowl with hot oatmeal porridge from the black iron kettle. Over it she dribbled a golden stream of treacle. Willie's mouth watered as he hopped up on the half-a-log bench behind the table.

"Eat up, lad," urged Mama, "for we be going on a far journey, me and thee."

Often Emily Adams used the quaint old English of her elderly parents, still asleep upstairs. Willie liked it. "Thee" and "thou" sounded nicer than just plain "you." And it seemed to suit his mother's tongue.

Pushing back his chair with a harsh scraping sound, Willie's father stood up. Henry Adams was a stockily-built man. He had steel-grey eyes, thick dark hair and beard and moustache, and large protruding ears that stuck out through bushy sideburns. His high forehead seemed always to be creased in a frown.

He spoke now for the first time since telling Samantha to scat. "I'll hitch Dobbin to the buggy while you and the boy breakfast." So saying, he lit a lantern and went out through the woodshed door to the barn. He was a man of few words, Henry Adams.

His breakfast done, Willie pulled his nightshirt off and began to dress in the clothes his mother had laid out for him. His Sunday-go-meeting suit! Where might they be going that he would need to wear his Sunday-go-meeting suit? And on a Thursday!

Stepping into the short stovepipe pants, Willie felt how good it was to be wearing real boy's clothes at last. Why, up until a month ago he'd worn nothing but frocks and rompers.

Now he stood between his mother's knees, in the drape of her long skirt, as she fixed his flaxen curls. Rubbing wet soap between her palms, she carefully plastered each curl around her index finger. Eleven long damp "sausages" she made that way. "Hold still until they dry," she cautioned.

Oh, how he hated those ringlets! But because he was the baby of the family, he knew it was his fate. It was common practice, in the year 1888, for doting mothers to keep their youngest overlong in frocks and curls. Even when the youngest was an impatient boy-child.

Chapter 2
A far journey

Presently Willie found himself wedged between his parents on the narrow buggy seat.

"Giddy-up!" called Papa to Dobbin, and the faithful workhorse started out at a slow trot.

The muddy wagon trail was shrouded in dense fog. Thunder rumbled in the distance. The deep forest pressed in around them.

"So dark it is," remarked Emily. "I can scarcely see my hand before my face."

Then Henry Adams slackened the reins, giving the horse its head. "No need to worry," he said gruffly, "Dobbin knows the road blindfold."

It had begun to rain, a soft warm drizzle. The curved roof of the buggy leaked. Willie felt damp and uncomfortable. He almost wished himself back at home in the crackly bed beside Artie.

Suddenly a flash of fork lightning pierced the murky sky. For a split-second they could see the road. They were passing Joseph Hickling's homestead. A lamp burned yellow in the window. The

Hicklings are up and about, thought Willie, so it must be five o'clock.

Daylight came slowly, held back by lowering clouds. Then, just as they neared the wayside station, the sun broke through. And at that very moment the Northern came whistling out of the wilderness.

Leaping from the buggy, Henry Adams ran to the tracks, flagging wildly with a big white handkerchief. The engineer, his striped cap poking out the little cab window, saw him just in time to grind the iron monster to a stop.

Shivers raced up Willie's spine. Was he really going somewhere on the train? His brother and sisters had been on train trips with their father, but because he was the youngest, he always had to stay home with Mama and Grandma and Grandpa.

"ALLABOOARD!" shouted the trainman.

The giant engine huffed and puffed. Steam billowed out from under the huge steel wheels. Willie felt Papa's strong hands lifting him up the high iron steps. A moment later he and Mama were waving goodbye out the rain-streaked window.

Slowly the train began to move. As it speeded up the wheels under the floorboards went clickety-clickety-clack. Outside, the misty forest went whizzing crazily by. Willie turned wide-eyed to look up at his mother.

She had taken her damp bonnet off. The sunbeams flitting through the window danced on her gold-plaited hair.

"Where are we going, Mama?" At last he could ask the all-important question.

"We be bound for Uncle Peter's house to care for Auntie Meg." She tucked a stray hairpin into the bun at the nape of her neck.

Uncle Peter was older brother to Mama and Uncle James. He and his wife lived in the far-off city of Toronto.

"Is Auntie Meg ailing, Mama?"

"In a manner of speaking, Willie, in a manner of speaking."

Satisfied, he began to look about. The high-backed seat they occupied was dark red plush. It had prickly horsehair stuffing that itched behind his knees.

The conductor came down the aisle, swaying expertly with the motion of the train. "Fares, please, ladies and gentlemen . . . have your fares ready!"

He pushed back the peak of his gold-braided cap with his thumb and winked at Willie as Mama paid their fare. Then he gave Willie a lemon drop.

Sucking happily on the bitter-sweet, Willie gazed out the window at the forest skimming by. Imagine! Himself — wee Willie Adams, who had never been farther yonder from home than the post office down the road — being off and away to Toronto!

The train made many stops along the way. Little groups of people gathered at wayside stations to wave at the lucky passengers. Willie waved back importantly.

At twelve o'clock they ate their noontime meal of fresh-baked bread and home-pressed cheese. Then, as the long day wore on, Willie grew weary. The steady motion of the coach and the singing of the rails finally lulled him off to sleep.

Suddenly he felt himself being shaken awake. "Willie!" he heard his mother calling. "Look alive, lad. We're here!"

Rubbing the sleep from his eyes, he gazed out the window. Sure enough, the train was chugging to a stop in front of a long station house with a big white sign which read PARKDALE STATION.

And there, pacing back and forth on the wide plank platform, was Uncle Peter.

Chapter 3
Lamplighter

The minute they arrived at Uncle Peter's house, Mama went straight upstairs. Willie was left sitting in the parlour. He was told, "Sit still and stay clean, there's a good boy."

Uncle Peter's house was very different from the loghouse. It had high ceilings, a red brick fireplace, and fancy furniture. Many pictures hung on twisted wires from the fuzzy-papered walls. One picture in particular caught Willie's attention. It was a water-colour in a carved oval frame of a pretty girl whose clear blue eyes seemed to follow him wherever he chanced to look.

He knew who the girl was because the exact same likeness hung in the parlour of the loghouse. It was a portrait of old Grandma when she was sixteen, his sister Nellie's age.

Willie tried to believe that old Grandma had once looked like that. But he couldn't. Where had her white teeth gone? Old Grandma had no teeth at all now and had to soak each crust of bread in her tea before she could swallow it. And what had happened to her sky-blue eyes? Old Grandma's eyes were all faded and sunken in. And her skin was as wrinkled and colourless as an old dishrag. How could those smooth pink cheeks ever have belonged to old Grandma?

After a long while his mother appeared at the parlour door. "Are thee famished, Willie?" she said. Then, not waiting for an answer, she set a cold supper on the tea table. But only the two of them sat down because Uncle Peter paced the floor and said he wasn't hungry.

Mama ate hurriedly, then, before Willie even had time to finish his seed cake, said, "Would thee like to sit out on the veranda a spell and watch the buggies go by?"

"Yes, Mama." He knew she wanted him out of the house but he didn't know why. Still, he didn't really mind because the parlour was a stuffy place and old Grandma's picture gave him a heartache.

His mother settled him on the veranda swing and gave him a peppermint stick to suck. "Now, then, hinny," she cautioned, "don't thee venture off the veranda. Toronto is a big place for a wee country boy to get himself lost in."

"I won't, Mama."

"There's a good lad. I'll come to fetch thee by and by."

The sun had not yet set behind the tall row of houses on the other side of the street. Ladies rocked to and fro on their verandas, fanning themselves with their handkerchiefs. Horses and buggies went clip-clopping down the cedar-block road. Young folk strolled arm in arm along the wooden sidewalk. The girls' petticoats made a rustling sound. A helmeted policeman passed by swinging his trusty billy.

Willie had never seen a city street before. So he went over to the railing to get a better look. All up and down on either side as far as the eye could see the houses were packed together like tall boxes lined up in a row.

He sat down again. Little by little the street became deserted. The sun was gone and there hadn't even been a sunset. What a strange place the city was. Why, back home in Muskoka the sunset's red glow lit up the sky for miles around.

Now it was quite dark. Willie glanced anxiously over his shoulder. Through the diamond-shaped windows he could see twin gas jets burning on the wall above the mantle. He decided to venture to the railing again.

Far down the long dark street he saw a light approaching. It seemed to be floating in the air. As it weaved its way up the street other lights sprang up behind it. I'm afeared! he thought, and went quickly back to the swing to tuck up his legs so he wouldn't be noticed. His peppermint stick had grown to a sharp point like an icicle. He sucked it carefully so as not to poke his tongue.

At last the mysterious light arrived at Uncle Peter's house. The torch carrier stretched his arm to the top of the lamppost that stood at the sidewalk's edge. The fire licked under the glass globe and burst into a white-hot flame.

Jabbing the pole into the lawn, the man mopped his brow with a big red handkerchief. As he did so he noticed the boy on the swing.

"Good evening to you, lad," he said politely.

"Good evening to you, sir," answered Willie. Then, encouraged by the stranger's friendly voice, he asked, "Who might you be?"

"Well, now, lad," chuckled the man, "I be the official lamplighter in these parts. I keep the city streets safe for folks to walk about at night."

"Oh, yes, it must be very safe now," agreed Willie, jumping up to the rail. "I can see you just as plain as day."

The lamplighter gave a hearty laugh, picked up his torch, and continued on his way. Willie watched in fascination as, one by one, the streetlamps glowed in the man's wake.

"Where art thou, wee Willie?" His mother had suddenly appeared in the doorway.

"Mama! Mama!" cried Willie, jumping backwards off the bottom rung, "I've seen the — "

"Hush!" His mother pressed a finger to her lips. "Come away in and see what I've been doing this long while."

Taking him by the hand, she led him into the shadowy hallway and up the carpeted staircase to a big square bedchamber. In a canopy bed under a lace counterpane, Auntie Meg lay pale but smiling. In the crook of her arm nestled a white cocoon with a tiny red face peeking out.

Uncle Peter stood at the head of the bed, his chest puffed out like a rooster. "Well, nipper," he beamed, his thumbs hooked into the armholes of his vest, "what do you think of your cousin, Emily?"

So that's what Mama had been doing this long while — helping Auntie Meg born Emily!

Willie crept closer. Emily was the smallest person he had ever seen. Her head was no bigger than his Christmas orange. One tiny fist opened like a rosebud. He slipped his finger in and five pink petals closed around it. His heart did somersaults.

"I *like* her," he declared.

Chapter 4
Home again

The trip home was long and tiresome. Across the aisle a fretful baby cried, giving Mama a headpain. She closed her eyes wearily and told Willie to look out the window. "There's a good boy."

Mile after mile, hour after hour, he stared out at the forest and the farmlands. At last the wayside station came in sight. And there was Papa, and Dobbin with the buggy. Leaping from the top of the train's high iron step, Willie ran towards them. "Halloo, Dobby!" he cried, reaching up to pat the horse's velvet nose. Dobby nickered and tossed his mane.

All the way home Mama talked about Auntie Meg and her new namesake, baby Emily. Willie had no chance to say a word. At last, round the bend and through the trees, the loghouse came in sight. And there was the whole family gathered outside to welcome them. Old Grandpa helped Mama down the buggy step, then he swung Willie clean off his feet. "Why, lad," he exclaimed, "you've got so big I'll wager you've gained a stone." He couldn't have said anything to please Willie more.

Then Willie ran to kiss old Grandma, who sat on a reed chair grinning from ear to ear with nary a tooth in sight. The girls hugged their mother as if she'd been gone a month, not just a week. Artie straddled the split-rail fence and threw his straw hat in the air. Uncle James was on hand, too. He had come for his annual summer visit.

Oh, it was good to be home again! And the log-house looked exactly the same as they'd left it. It wasn't a grand house like Uncle Peter's, to be sure. But it was cosy, and it smelled of pine scent, and it was home.

Nellie had the supper on, so they all sat down around the big board table. The children were all laughing and talking at once but on this special occasion Papa didn't reprimand them.

Suddenly Uncle James cleared his throat with a loud "harrumph!" and all eyes swung towards him. "Well, young man," he said to Willie, "have you decided yet what you're going to be when you grow up?"

Now all eyes turned towards Willie. But this time he didn't hang his head. Instead he looked Uncle James straight in the eye and replied in a clear, confident voice, "When I be a man, I'm going to be a lamplighter. I'm going to keep the city streets safe for folks to walk about at night."

Alice and Nellie and May and Mama all cried "Ohhh!" And old Grandma's faded eyes lit up at the news. "Mine own dear faither was a lamplighter in Nottingham when I was a wee bit girl," she said. Artie just sat with mouth agape and didn't make a sound.

"Well, bless my soul," declared Uncle James, his brown eyes twinkling. "Whatever gave you that idea?"

Then at last Willie was able to tell them all about his adventures on the veranda while little Emily was being born.

Darkness crept into the old loghouse. A lamp was lit and placed upon the table. Then Henry Adams spoke for the first time since the travellers returned.

"Well, boy," he said in his usual gruff manner, "since you've a mind to be a lamplighter when you grow up, it's high time you had some practice." So saying, he went to the sideboard drawer and drew out a new white candle and handed it to Willie. "You may light it yourself and carry it to bed tonight."

Willie could scarcely believe his ears.

Artie was furious. "*I* couldn't light my own

candle until I was eight years old!" he cried indignantly.

"Hold your tongue," growled Papa.

"Ah, yes," put in Uncle James, "but you're not going to be a lamplighter when you grow up."

Everyone laughed, save Artie, who wore a sullen scowl.

"Thank you, Papa," said Willie, accepting the candle, "And thank you, too, Mama, for taking me to the city."

"You're welcome indeed, wee Willie. But I musn't call you 'wee' any-the-more. And tomorrow off come your curls." She pulled one of the "sausages" and let it bob back like a coiled spring. "A lad who has his future mapped is too much a man for ringlets!"

Willie's heart jumped for joy.

Now, with all eyes upon him, he climbed up on the half-a-log bench and held the tip of his candle over the lamp's glass chimney. Instantly a bright flame shot up. Just like the gas lamp when the lamplighter touched it with his torch, thought Willie.

Holding the glowing taper proudly aloft, he called out triumphantly, "Goodnight everyone!" Then he disappeared up the dark stairwell.

Chapter 5
Danger on the path

The last day of September was a beautiful autumn day. And it was Willie's birthday. He was seven years old. First thing that morning his mother measured him against the wall. But when he stepped away to see how high he was, he was disappointed. This year's mark was almost in the same place as last year's mark.

"I didn't grow, Mama!"

"Well, then, it's more turnips for you, my lad."

"But I don't like turnips!"

"Turnips be good growing vegetables, Willie. Do you mind the time the frost took Myrtle Hickling's garden? Everything was spoiled except the turnips. And that very year young Jamie Hickling grew four inches. In just one year, mind you. And all he had to eat was turnips all winter long."

"Oh, all right, Mama," sighed Willie. "I'll eat my turnips."

"There's a good wee lad," said Mama, forgetting about the 'wee.' "And I'll make thee lovely turnip things, you'll see. We'll have turnip cake and turnip pie and mayhap even turnip pudding. Why, you'll hardly know what you're eating."

Willie knew if anyone could make turnips taste good his mother could. But he also knew that the frost had took their vegetable patch and his mother was trying hard to make the best of it.

That afternoon he asked, "What can we do for my birthday, Mama?"

"Well, now, love," Emily covered a bowl of rising dough with a clean white sugar bag, "what would thee like to do?"

"May we go to the post, me and thee?"

His mother laughed to hear the old-fashioned phrase coming from her little boy's lips. "That sounds grand, Willie. It's been ages since I've had a chat with Maudie."

Maudie Hanley was the postmistress for the tiny hamlet of Elderberry. She was also his mother's lifelong friend. Their two families had been the very first settlers of that remote Muskoka region.

The post office was a mile and a half down a wild and woodsy wagon trail. A tunnel of red and gold leaves glittered overhead in the sunlight. Flaming sumach seemed to set the bush afire. Willie skipped along as happy as a bluejay in a red-berried hawthorn tree.

At last the post office came in sight and there

sat Maudie on a log bench, her face upturned to the sun. When she heard their footsteps crunching through the leaves she jumped up and ran to meet them. Grasping Willie by the hands, she flew him around in a wide circle like a bird on a string. "Land-o-goshen but you're a welcome sight!" she cried. Then she slipped her arm through Emily's and led the way to where she lived in the back room behind the post office. She threw a log on the fire, put the kettle on to boil, and gave Willie a home-made maple sugar patty for his birthday.

Willie sat himself down in a corner on a milking stool and coaxed Maudie's big orange cat up on his lap. Tom was a strange cat who wagged his tail like a dog. Maudie said that was because Tom had been raised by a collie.

Willie nibbled the patty slowly, round and round the edge, while Maudie and his mother chatted over their tea. He tried not to interrupt because he knew how much these rare visits meant to his mother. His father was a quiet man, and old Grandma didn't chat much any more.

All too soon it was time to leave.

Just as they were bidding Maudie goodbye at the door she threw up her hands and exclaimed, "Oh, my land I near forgot!" In a flurry she disappeared behind the post office wicket. Then she reappeared waving a brown paper parcel. "It's a package for you, Willie; it came in this morning's post."

Willie reached for the package, his eyes as big as saucers. Never in his life before had he received a parcel in the post. There was neat black printing on the label. "What does it say, Mama?" he asked breathlessly.

"Well, bless my soul," exclaimed Mama. "It says 'Master William Adams, Elderberry Post Office, Muskoka, Ontario.' Now, I wonder who would be sending thee a parcel?"

"Oh, let's go home, Mama. I want to open it at home."

So off they went with Maudie calling wistfully after them, "Don't be strangers now!"

"Hurry, Mama," begged Willie, for she kept stopping along the way to gather autumn leaves. So they quickened their pace as the September sun began to hide behind the trees. Already crickets had begun their evening song. Willie leaned down to catch one big black fellow as it chirped shrilly from a rock, but it sprang away into the underbrush. Then just as he was straightening up he spied something brown and fluffy down the road.

His mother saw it too and stopped in her tracks.

"What is it, Mama?"

" 'Tis a wee bear cub."

"A bear cub!" Willie was just about to dart

towards it when his mother grasped him by the arm. "Don't thee move a muscle!" she commanded in a sharp whisper.

Weaving its head and sniffing the air, the baby bear gazed in their direction.

"He's caught our scent," murmured Mama. "Come, Willie. Very slowly now, walk backwards step by step. We must put as much distance as we can between us."

"Why, Mama? He looks too wee to hurt us."

"Aye," agreed his mother, "but his mama is big and strong."

"Is he lost, Mama?"

"No, Willie, mamas don't lose their babies. She'll not be far away."

The little fellow came waddling towards them, making squeaky baby sounds.

"He's not a bit afeared, Mama," whispered Willie.

"No, hinny. He's too young to fear our human scent, and curious to know what sort of creatures we might be." She tightened her grip on his arm. "Hush now, no more talking."

As they continued backtracking, Emily searched the woods with anxious eyes. "A wee lad would be safer in a tree," she murmured. But, alas, on this lonely stretch of road only giant jack pines and towering spruce trees grew.

Suddenly, from out of the forest came a loud crashing of underbrush. With a rumbling roar the wild mother bounded into sight. Rising on hind legs, huge and powerful, she sniffed the air for danger while her rambunctious offspring bounced joyously around her. Dropping to all fours, she nuzzled him from tip to tail, making sure no harm had come to him. Then she raised her shaggy head and looked directly at Willie and his mother.

They stood stock-still, the brave pioneer woman hiding her son behind her in the folds of her long black skirt. Then out of the corner of his eye Willie spied a big, thick stick with a knobby end like a club. In one swift motion he grabbed it up and stepped in front of his mother. She gasped and gripped him by the shoulders. "Still! Still, little one. Very still," she whispered urgently.

They did not blink or even dare to breathe.

The mother bear ambled closer, her saucy son gambolling around her. With near-sighted eyes she looked towards them and sniffed the air.

Then, for no apparent reason, she swung about, gave a loud grunt, and lumbered off into the forest. With a plaintive cry that sounded like "Wait for me!" the baby bear went scrambling after her.

Willie and his mother did not stir until the sound of the bears crashing through the forest had faded into the distance.

Then Emily drew in a deep breath and let it out in a low sigh. "Well, Willie, my lad," she said in her own natural voice, "and what did thee think of the bears?"

"Oh, weren't they lovely bears, Mama! I wish I could catch the little one and take him home to be my pet."

"Bears be darlin' creatures, Willie, but they belong in the woods and not about the house." She pointed, then, to Willie's stick. "And what did you intend to do with that, pray?"

He held it up and swung the knobby end. "If she had attacked us, Mama, I meant to save you. I would have beat her on the head until she fell dead, so I would."

"Thou art brave but foolhardy, Willie. No one, not even thy Papa, is strong enough to fight a bear. So let this be a lesson to you, lad: when there is no escape the wisest thing to do is to blend into the landscape. Be still as a rock. Do you heed me?"

"Yes, Mama." Then he said thoughtfully. "The baby bear is lucky to have such a nice mama to take care of him."

"He is that, Willie."

"So am I, Mama."

She looked down and their eyes met and they exchanged a wonderful smile. "And 'tis a lucky woman I am," she added, "to have such a brave son to defend me."

Willie whacked the stick against a tree and laughed proudly, and they hurried home in the twilight.

Chapter 6
Happy birthday, Willie!

Nellie had the supper on and Papa was washing up at the basin when Willie and his mother came rushing in the door.

Willie could hardly eat a bite for talking about the bears. His father grumbled that so much prattle would give a man a headpain. His mother told him "Hush!" time and time again, but Willie did not hush until Papa cracked his knuckles with a spoon. Then he dropped his eyes to hide the tears and did not look up again until Nellie brought a lighted cake from the pantry.

"Happy birthday, Willie!" chorused his family.

"Don't forget to make a wish," reminded Alice.

He closed his eyes and wished fervently that he would grow four inches in just one year like Jamie Hickling. Then he took a deep breath and blew out all seven candles in one huff. Nellie cut the cake in squares and Mama served it up. Old Grandma smacked her lips while she waited, then sucked her portion in with toothless gums.

When every crumb was gone Mama handed Willie his parcel from the post. Eagerly he tore the wrappings off and found inside a brand-new game of checkers and a hand-painted card of a bluebird sitting on a twig. (Auntie Meg was known for her artistic talent.) Inside, the card read, "To Wee Willie, with much love, from your tiny cousin, Emily."

"A game! A game!" cried Willie. "Will you play it with me, Artie, afore we go to bed?"

Surprised, Artie could only nod his head.

Everyone in the family had a gift for him. From his parents came a pair of high-button boots and a steel buttonhook to fasten them. May gave him a real school slate. Not a new one, but it was black and shiny as new.

"Thank you, May. But I don't know how to write."

"I'll teach you, Willie," promised his sister.

Nellie presented him with a picture book called *Animals Of The Wild*. It wasn't new, either. Inside the front cover, written in scrolly script, were the words, "To Nellie Adams, for good behaviour and regular attendance at Elderberry Church, Christmas, 1882." Under it Nellie had written in a schoolgirl hand, "To my little brother, Willie, on his seventh birthday, from your loving sister, Nell. September 30, 1888."

"My very own picture book!" exclaimed Willie. "I'll try to keep it perfect all my life."

Alice had sewn him four white handkerchiefs from an empty flour bag. In the corners she had embroidered his initials, W.H.A. (William Henry Adams — after Papa). It made him feel suddenly important.

Even Artie had a gift for him. It was a little blue wooden box. "To keep your treasures in," explained the older boy. "It's just an old cigar box Uncle James left behind. I sanded it smooth and painted it myself."

"It's grand, Artie!" Willie was overwhelmed. "I'll keep all my treasures in it all my life."

Last of all, old Grandpa came forward and pressed a silver dime into his grandson's hand. "From Grandma and me," he said simply, patting Willie's head. Willie thanked him with a tight hug, then went over to the daybed and kissed old Grandma's withered cheek. He was beginning to feel like a greedy boy to have so many gifts.

He tucked the dime carefully inside his treasure chest, and when he went off to bed he shoved the box under the washstand. Then he knelt to say his prayers. "Thank you for my birthday, God. It was the best ever. Bless the baby bear and his mother and keep them safe in the forest. And bless all my family." He blew out the candle and climbed into the crackly bed.

Outside the window a hoot owl called, "Who! Who! Who!"

Willie laughed and answered, "Me! Me! Me!" It was grand to be seven years old.

Chapter 7
Layabout?

One cold November morning Willie woke to find that Jack Frost had been busy in the night. The windowpane was painted with a snow-white frosty forest.

Artie was up and about, so Willie had the bed to himself. He stretched his legs and laughed out loud as the cornhusks snapped and crackled.

Outside the icy window he could hear the chop, chop, chop of the axe. His father spoke and old Grandpa answered, but Willie could not tell what they were saying. From the kitchen below came the hum of voices and the clatter of pots and pans.

I'd best get up and help with the chores, he thought as he snuggled deeper under the patchwork quilt. He knew his mother was letting him lie abed until the cookstove made the kitchen warm and cosy. His father said he was a molly-coddle and he would become a layabout. But his mother said no, her Willie was a good wee lad. With a sigh Willie jumped out of bed, dressed in a wink, and hurried down the stairs.

Old Grandpa and Papa were just coming in the door, their arms loaded with kindling. The cold air whistled in around them.

"Eeeeh!" complained old Grandma, drawing her black woolen shawl closer around her bony shoulders. "Another winter will surely be the death of me."

Willie sat behind the table on the half-a-log bench, spooning in his porridge. How he wished that he was big enough to ride in the wagon behind Dobbin to the forest back of the house to help fell the trees for winter fuel.

Now Artie was putting on his coat and cap to go with Papa because old Grandpa was winded and needed a respite. So Willie decided to speak. "Papa . . ."

Henry Adams paused with his hand upon the latch. "What is it, boy?"

"Papa," Willie hurried on before he lost his courage, "may I please go with you and Artie to help chop down the trees?"

"No," answered his father abruptly. "You'd be nothing but a hindrance."

"No, I wouldn't, Papa!" protested Willie.

"Learn to speak when you are spoken to," his father snapped. Then he marched out the door with Artie hard on his heels. But before Artie disappeared he managed to shoot his little brother a mocking backward glance.

"Why don't Papa and Artie like me, Mama?" Willie sighed.

"They do, hinny, they do. But they don't know how to show it, more's the pity. They're alike as two peas in a pod."

Artie has an odd way to show it, thought Willie as he rubbed his ears, which were still smarting from what had happened to them yesterday.

It wasn't until Mama had cut off his curls that Artie had noticed what large ears Willie had. "Big as handles on a chamber pot," sneered the older boy. Then he had called him Mama's sucky-baby and grabbed him by the offending ears and flung him over the split-rail fence. "And if you dare to tattle," he had glowered menacingly, "I'll throw you o'er the house next time!"

I wish I didn't get Papa's big ears, thought Willie, glaring at the woodshed door, 'cause Artie hurts me when he flings me o'er the fence.

"Why are you pulling your lugs, hinny?" Mama asked suddenly. When he didn't answer she leaned over the table and touched them, causing him to wince. "Why, they're all red and swollen. Whatever happened?"

"I can't tell you, Mama."

"Why ever not, pray?"

"Because . . . because . . . Artie says if I tattle, next time he'll throw me o'er the housetop."

"He'll do no such thing. Now out with it."

So Willie told, and Mama frowned in pain. "He'll not do that again, son, never fear. Your father will put a spoke in his wheel." But Willie, still feeling sorry for himself, went behind the stove to sulk.

Turning her attention to the butter crock, Emily began scraping it down with a wooden paddle. "There's nary a smidgen left," she remarked. "I'll be needing to use the big wooden churn this day." Dragging the heavy churn from the corner, she continued to speak as if to herself. "The livestock want to be fed and I don't know where I'll find the time. Nellie and May are up to their elbows in soapsuds, Alice is giving Grandma a sponge bath, and Grandpa is busy mending a hole in the softwater pail. Now I wonder who could feed the animals?"

"I'll do it, Mama!" Willie scrambled out from behind the stove. "Let me!"

"Why, thank you, hinny. That'll be a real fine help, so it will."

Willie dressed quickly in his cap and muffler and set off for the barn.

"Don't forget to feed Gertie!" his mother called

after him as a gust of wind slammed the woodshed door between them.

Chapter 8
Mother Nature

From deep in the woods he heard the fall of the axe ringing through the trees. His father's harsh words were still ringing in his ears. So, to take his mind away, he called for Sam to follow. "Here kitty, kitty!" he coaxed.

The path to the barn sparkled with icy morning dew. Sam started after him, but the hoar frost nipped her tender paws and made her change her mind. Turning tail, she ran yowling back to the woodshed.

Willie pulled his muffler up against the cold wind. "Wind from the east, not fit for beast. Wind from the west is always best," he sang as he chanted old Grandpa's rhyme.

Inside, the barn felt warm and pleasant after the windswept barnyard. Yet the cow in her stall had frosty mist swirling about her nostrils.

"Hello, there, Bessie. Are you cold today?"

She answered him in a soft, lowing moo.

"Chook! Chook! Chook!" called Willie as he scattered seed over the old barn floor. The hens came cackling from their nests and Gertie the goose flew honking from the haymow. Willie stood quite still until all the seed was gone. Then the saucy goose, her hunger not yet satisfied, flapped her wide wings and darted at him with her long neck outstretched.

His father and Artie called Gertie a mean old bird. But she never pecked at Willie the way she did at them. She followed him now to the pigpen and strutted about as he tickled the fat sow's stomach. The sow snuffled happily and Willie told her what a nice old pig she was. Then Gertie bunted him jealously with her hard black beak. "I love you, too, Gertie, indeed I do," he laughed, stroking her silver feathers. He held out a few kernels of corn and she snapped them up greedily without nipping his hand.

Animals are nice, thought Willie. They never treat you horrid. If you be friends with them, they'll be friends with you.

* * *

Directly after the noonday meal Henry Adams and his oldest son set off for Huntsville to fetch their winter supplies. Soon the heavy snows would come and they'd be winterbound in the old loghouse.

Willie wished that he, too, could go to town and help load the wagon. But he watched them leave and didn't say a word.

"Have you any more chores for me to do,

Mama?" He was determined to prove that he was not a layabout.

"I'll be needing fresh water from the spring," she said as she set the wooden cheesepress on the table. "Half a bucket will do fine, hinny. A full bucket is too much for thee to carry up the hill."

There were times when his mother wished they had a well in their front yard like some of their neighbours. "What a fine thing it would be," she said, "just to pump a handle and fill a pail and bring it right into the house." But their father said it was healthful for the children to fetch water up the hill. It would make men and women out of them.

Down the winding footpath, about fifty yards below the house, the spring bubbled pure and clear. Willie skippety-hopped down the path, swinging the pail at his side. A little chipmunk skittered out of the brush. Willie felt in his pocket and dropped a few seeds on the ground. Quick as a flash the tiny creature filled its pouches and scurried away into the bush.

Before he could see it with his eyes, Willie could hear the spring. It gurgled out of the frozen earth into a wooden tub. And at that very moment a dappled fawn was drinking its fill from the tub. Willie stood stock-still. How beautiful the baby deer was. He'd like to stand there and watch it for hours. But the fawn raised its graceful head and saw him. For a split-second their eyes met — the blue eyes of the boy and the brown eyes of the fawn — then she took flight. She darted away on spindly legs and disappeared into the safety of the forest.

Dipping the pail into the tub, Willie filled it to the brim. Then he heaved it a few steps at a time back up the hill. As he neared the house he spied a roly-poly porcupine nibbling on the corner of the woodshed. Willie liked him, too, but he knew you could not make friends with a porcupine. Old Grandpa said porkies were something to be reckoned with. This one soon caught his scent and scrambled off into the woods to join his wild brothers and sisters.

"Oh, my, what a fine big bucketful!" exclaimed Mama as Willie lowered it, panting, to the floor.

"Guess what I saw, Grandpa," he cried excitedly. "A big fat porcupine nibbling on the woodshed."

"I'll have to drench a stump with salt to lure him away," said Grandpa.

"You're ever so clever, Grandpa," admired Willie.

"You live and learn, lad, you live and learn," answered the old man. "I mind the time — "

But before he could launch into his story his wife broke in.

"I want this here toadstool took off my face,"

she demanded, stroking a large brown mole on her chin. Out of the lumpy growth sprouted two curly black hairs. Willie thought it looked like a bug with feelers.

"Why, that's no trick at all," said Emily. She reached for her sewing basket from on top of the cupboard, then hunted up black thread and scissors. "Now, you just hold still, Muma," she said.

Willie and Alice and May gathered around to watch. The mole quivered as the old lady jutted out her bristly chin. Her daughter circled it with the thread and tied it tightly with a slip-knot. Then she snipped off the dangling thread with the scissors. "There, now," Emily nodded sagely. "Don't wash your face for a week, Muma, and it'll fall right off, so it will."

Alice was fascinated. "What will make it drop off, Mama?"

"The thread stops the circulation and the mole dies, hinny. And your Grandma won't feel a thing."

Sure enough, a week to the day, the ugly mole fell right into old Grandma's broth, thread and all. Papa gagged loudly and said it was enough to turn a man's stomach.

That night, with the chores all done and Artie and Papa not yet home, old Grandpa said, "This seems like a fine time for a story." So saying he went to the parlour and brought back one of his leather-bound books. The name of the book was, *Stories for Leisure Hours*. It was seldom opened.

Sitting at the table by the oil lamp, Grandpa read a fable about a wicked boy who stole apples because he was hungry. And he received a terrible caning for his crime. (Willie knew what a caning felt like because when he was four years old he'd wet his drawers and Papa had caned him to teach him a lesson.) The old man read with such expression, having been a schoolmaster in Nottingham when he was young, that Willie trembled in sympathy for the boy. And he vowed never again to steal rhubarb from the garden.

"One more story. Please, Grandpa!" he begged, squeezing into his grandfather's chair. The old man shifted over and put his arm around his grandson. Then he turned the page and read "The Widow's Lamp." It was a tale about a poor widow whose cottage was on the seashore. " . . . And many a ship was wrecked on that rugged coast, so the woman placed her lamp on the window ledge and the flickering light warned the mariners on dark and stormy nights. And many a seaman's life was saved by the kindly widow's lamp."

Willie sighed contentedly with the happy ending as Grandpa closed the book. Then the old folks took themselves off to bed, and so did Willie because he was weary from all the work he'd done that day.

He fell asleep instantly and dreamed it was summertime. In his dream he was going to the post office all by himself. Suddenly it was very dark and he found to his surprise that he was carrying a torch. Then he noticed that there were gas lamps tucked among the trees. He began darting back and forth like a white-tailed deer, lighting lamps all along the way. It was a lovely dream, and in the morning he was disappointed to find himself clinging to the edge of the crackly mattress beside Artie.

When he went downstairs, he saw that his father was still breakfasting at the head of the table. So he slipped quietly into his place on the half-a-log bench.

Without a word, Henry Adams placed a big brown copper beside his son's porridge bowl. Willie regarded the money uncertainly. He raised his eyes and met his father's gaze. "Your mother says you worked like a man yesterday," said Henry. "And I say a man deserves to be paid." Immediately he scraped back his chair, grabbed his coat, and was out the door. Willie had no chance to say thank you. But his chest swelled with pride. His father had called him a man!

Chapter 9
Christmas Eve

On the morning of Christmas Eve, Willie was allowed, for the first time ever, to go with his father and brother to help choose the Yuletide tree. The three of them set off in the sleigh behind a frisky Dobbin. Over the crisp white snow they skimmed to the forest at the back of the house. When they were deep in the woods Papa called "Whoa!" and Dobbin stopped in a flurry of sparkling snow.

Jumping from the sleigh (it was a low sleigh with wooden runners close to the ground), Willie made straight for a bushy pine. "Here's one, Papa!" he cried excitedly.

"That won't do!" called his father, "Our tree must be tall as well as wide."

"This one's tall, Papa!" Artie stood knee-deep in a snowdrift squinting up at a scraggly spruce.

"That won't do either," rejected Henry Adams bluntly. "Our tree must be perfect in shape."

"Here's a beauty one, Papa," Willie pointed hopefully at a handsome hemlock.

"Use your head, boy. Hemlocks are too easily set afire."

Crestfallen, Willie wandered some thirty paces away. Suddenly he found himself standing beside a perfect balsam. "I've found it, Papa!" he yelled. "I've found our tree."

Papa and Artie came running and Dobbin whinnied and tossed his mane.

Sizing the balsam up and down from top to bottom, Henry Adams slowly nodded his head. "Aye," he agreed, " 'tis our tree right enough."

With three quick strokes of the axe the lovely balsam came crashing to the ground. Panting and laughing together they loaded it onto the sleigh. Snow and all they hauled their prize into the old pine kitchen. "Ohhh!" cried Mama, and "Eeeeh!" cried Grandma, and the three girls clapped their hands ecstatically. Then Papa made a wooden stand and stood the tree upright in the corner.

In the afternoon, when all the chores were done, the five children gathered around their father's workbench. He sat on a wooden stool by the woodshed door, cobbling boots.

Because she was the eldest, Nellie was their spokesman. "Papa," she began. He took a tack from his mouth and pounded it into the rubber heel. "Papa," she repeated.

"Mmmm?" he muttered through a row of tacks pursed between his lips.

"May we have the parlour stove lit now? We have a special task to do today."

He spat the tacks into a box, set the iron last and boot on the bench, and led the way to the parlour.

Except on rare occasions the parlour was not used. The door latch made a grating sound that set their teeth on edge. Then a cold draught rushed into the kitchen as the door creaked open.

"Eeeeh!" cried old Grandma, covering up her head. "I'll surely ketch me death of py-nee-monia!"

Inside, the children huddled together while their father set about lighting the potbellied stove.

Pale sunlight filtered through the one narrow window. Willie squinted in the dimness and let his eyes roam about the room. It was almost as strange a place as if it was in someone else's house. The furniture was unfamiliar: a spinet, a settle, and a small octagonal table with a shaded oil lamp on it. A braided rag mat covered the centre of the floor.

Above a dusty spinning wheel hung a sampler in a crisscross frame. Alice strained her eyes and read it aloud.

" 'A good man is a diamond; a good woman is a pearl; but there is no stone so precious, as a good boy or a girl. By Emily Swift, eight years and four months old.' Ah, imagine Mama doing such fine needlework when she was a wee bit girl."

The fire began to crackle and the room warmed slowly. Without a backward glance Henry Adams went out and shut the door, leaving his children to their secrets.

"Quickly!" Nellie clapped her hands excitedly, "Empty your pockets into the pan."

They turned their pockets inside out, dropping bits of yellow tallow into the pot until it was almost full. Then Nellie placed the saucepan on the hot stove lid. Instantly the wax began to melt like snow on a warm spring day.

All year long they had been secretly saving the drippings from their bedtime candles. Now they had enough to make a brand-new candle for their mother's Christmas gift.

While the girls were busy candle-making, the boys set about their special task. Just that morning Willie had plucked from Gertie's wing her finest silver feather. The indignant goose had honked in protest, but she hadn't tried to bite him.

Sitting on a stool by the dingy window, Willie brushed Gertie's plume until it shone like silk. Then Artie trimmed and honed it with his pocketknife and whetstone. When he was finished the feather's point was as fine and sharp as a needle.

At last their work was done and they placed the gifts upon the table for each other to admire.

"Oh, the candle's beautiful!" exclaimed Willie. It was cloudy-white and streaky-red from elderberry dye.

"Mama will surely never burn it," declared Artie.

"Well, Papa will write a lovely clear hand in his journal with this fine quill," remarked Nellie. May and Alice bobbed their heads in agreement.

They had presents for the old folks, too. The night before, after their grandparents had gone to bed, the girls had made soft maple-cream for toothless old Grandma, and the boys had sanded pieces of pinewood smooth as satin for old Grandpa's favourite pastime — whittling.

"It's getting cold in here," shivered May.

"Aye," agreed Nellie. "Let's wrap the gifts afore the fire goes out."

They wrapped them neatly in pages from last year's *Farmer's Journals* and tied them with bright red yarn.

"There, now!" Nellie breathed a sigh of satisfaction. "Let the Yuletide come!"

Christmas Eve! The bells rang out from the old stone church built by pioneers like Grandma and Grandpa from the stones cleared off their land. The whole family bundled into the sleigh to join the carol singing with their neighbours.

Then, the minute they got home again, Willie asked eagerly, "Is it time yet, Mama?"

" 'Tis time, indeed, little one. Old Saint Nick will be here before we know it." From her sewing basket she handed each of her children a long black stocking.

Up the narrow stairs they trooped to hang the well-darned stockings on the iron bedstead posts.

Shivering in their nightshirts and matching caps, Willie and Artie peeked through the cracks in the chinking. If only they could catch one glimpse of Santa on his sleigh! But the stinging wind whistled through the cracks, blinding their eyes with tears. So they jumped into bed and the cornhusks snapped and crackled from the cold.

"Artie," Willie's voice was troubled, "are you sure Santa knows where we live?"

"Of course, you dolt. Go to sleep."

"Does he have to visit the city first?"

"I expect so."

"Then there might be nothing left in his sack by the time he gets here. Elderberry is such a wee little place. Mayhap he won't see it from high up in the sky."

"All my life he has never failed to come," grumbled the older boy. But he wished Willie would not put such doubts into his head!

"But, Artie . . . "

"Go to sleep, I say!"

His brother's cross voice made Willie hold his tongue.

Edging as close as he dared to Artie for warmth, he finally fell asleep to dream of sleigh bells and reindeer prancing on the roof.

Chapter 10
Yuletide table

Dawn crept in through the frozen windowpane. Willie woke with a start. His heart pounding, he stretched his hand towards the bedstead post. A thrill went quivering through him as he felt the toe of his stocking bulging with strange lumps and bumps.

"Artie! Artie! Santa's come! It's Christmas!" He had no fear of waking his big brother on Christmas Day. Even though Artie was eleven years old and worked like a man with his father and grandfather in the fields, still, on this special day he was a child again.

They shook their stockings on the quilt and out rolled two sunny oranges (the first since Christmas last), two bright red apples, and filberts and walnuts that clacked against each other. But something was stuck in the stockings' legs. They gave hard shakes and out popped peppermint sticks, red and white and long enough to last all day if you sucked them slow.

Through the thin wall they could hear their sisters' happy voices. Then all five of them trooped down the stairs, their treasures in their arms, shouting, "Merry Christmas!" Even Nellie, who was sixteen past, felt like a little girl again on Christmas Day.

The old pine kitchen was gay with smiles and laughter. The perfect balsam shimmered in the lamplight. Its homemade trimmings of coloured yarn, painted pine-cones, and loops of popcorn garlands made a lovely sight to see. And under its spreading branches were tucked the Christmas gifts.

But first breakfast must be eaten. It was their father's rule.

At last it was time. From Papa's hand each child received his treasure. For Willie it was a thick writing tablet and a brand-new pencil not yet sharpened.

"Whittle it for me, Grandpa," he cried excitedly. And with his pocketknife the old man shaved the long red pencil into a perfect point.

Old Grandma had knit the whole family woolen toques and scarves and mittens. Willie's were bright red. How had she managed such a task with her gnarled rheumatic fingers?

Now, beside themselves with excitement, the children presented the presents they had made.

They held their breath as Mama untied the red yarn bow and the pages fell away. Her hand flew to her mouth. "Ohhh!" she cried, tears springing to her eyes. " 'Tis too beautiful . . . much too beautiful to burn!"

"We knew you'd say that, Mama! We knew you'd say that!" chorused her children. She laughed and brushed the tears away and thanked them with a kiss.

Then it was Papa's turn. But when he opened up his parcel he didn't seem to know what to do. So he tested the sharp quill with a calloused fingertip; he held the glossy feather up to the light, turning it this way and that; but he did not know how to thank his children.

Suddenly he stood up and went to the sideboard drawer, withdrew his daily journal, opened up a pot of ink upon the table, and dipped in the quill's fine point. His children peered eagerly over his shoulders to see what he would write. "On this Christmas Day in the year of our Lord, 1888, my children, Nellie, May, Alice, Arthur and William, presented to me, Henry Adams, Esquire, this most excellent goosequill pen."

Old Grandma had already torn open her present and gobbled it up until every lick was gone.

From his Christmas box old Grandpa selected a perfect block of pine. Snapping open his knife he began to whittle. In minutes a miniature reindeer took shape.

All afternoon Willie sat in the cosy spot behind the stove, sucking on his peppermint stick and scribbling in his tablet. "Mayhap I won't need to go to school, Mama. May says I can read and write better than most of the girls and boys in third book."

"That's because your sister is such a good teacher, Willie. But do you know your sums?"

"No," he had to admit, "Well, then, when can I go to school?"

"Soon, little one, very soon." Emily pared the potatoes paper thin and chopped up a huge yellow turnip. "The schoolhouse is a far piece down the road. And the snowdrifts would be well over thy head, so they would. Perhaps you'd best stay home another year."

Willie was disappointed. He did so want to be grown-up like his brother and sisters. And much as he loved his mother, he didn't want to be her baby any-the-more. But soon he forgot all about school as the kitchen began to fill with lovely cooking smells. The plum pudding was bubbling in the pot, and Mama hummed a Yuletide hymn as she stirred the sugar sauce.

Willie's stomach began to grumble, and old Grandma's anxious tongue darted in and out. Artie watched hungrily as his sisters laid the table with the white linen cloth and Grandma's precious china (brought all the way from Nottingham so many years ago). Artie and old Grandpa pushed the chairs up to the table. Papa raised his eyes from the workbench and sniffed the delicious aromas.

Spread out on the bench in front of him were the parts and pieces and watchbob of a gold timepiece that belonged to Joseph Hickling. It was well-known thereabouts that Henry Adams was clever with his hands. ("If Henry can't fix it, it's broke for sure," his wife was often heard to say.) In this way he earned an extra dollar for his family.

At last it was time to gather round the board.

With bowed heads and folded hands, they waited as Papa said the blessing. Then all eyes followed Mama to the stove. Leaning down, a folded flannel in each hand, she lifted the Yuletide fowl, all golden-brown and shining, from the oven.

Willie's bright eyes fastened eagerly on the lovely glistening bird. Then his smile vanished and his heart gave a sickening thud. Suddenly, in his mind's eye, he saw Gertie, her silver wings flapping from the haymow. Gertie! Was it Gertie that his father was just about to slice? Why, t'was only yesterday that she had given him her very finest feather! For Papa's plume!

"Mama! Mama! Is it Gertie? Are we going to eat my Gertie?"

"Hush now, lad." His mother's voice was firm but gentle. "Remember, Willie, that's what geese be for."

Frantically Willie scrambled out from his place behind the table. "I won't eat Gertie!" he screamed furiously. "I won't eat my friend!"

"*SIT YE DOWN!*" commanded his father in a fearful booming voice. "Ye'll eat and be thankful."

But Willie ran stumbling to the stairwell, tears raining down his face. "No! No! NO!" he shrieked.

"Then get ye to bed, ungrateful boy, and leave us to our supper."

Over the Yuletide table there fell a dreadful hush. Old Grandma whimpered pitifully and old Grandpa whispered, "Shush!" The children stared, wide-eyed, at their little brother who dared to disobey their father.

Willie's hand was on the door latch when his mother spoke. Her voice was soft and low, but in that silent room it could be plainly heard.

"Mr. Adams," — she only addressed her husband as Mister when she was very, very vexed — "no child of mine shall miss his Christmas repast." Then she held out her hand to her defiant son. "Come, Willie, sit thyself down. You need not eat the goose this day."

Now all eyes turned towards the father. He stood, stone-faced, knife in hand, as his wayward son returned trembling to the table. Under his steely gaze the boy felt very, very wee.

"Give me your plate!" commanded the father.

Willie's hand shook so badly that he came near to dropping old Grandma's precious china.

Henry Adams took the plate, then, very deliberately, filled it to the brim . . . from the turnip bowl!

"What do you say to that then?" he demanded, holding the pungent yellow mound right under Willie's nose.

The only sound that could be heard was the ticking of the clock. In a small voice, Willie answered, "Thank you, Papa." Then he piled high his spoon with turnip, placed it in his mouth, and swallowed hard. Now he raised his tear-stained face and looked straight into his father's eyes. "The turnips are lovely!" he declared.

Suddenly the hush was shattered by gales of helpless laughter.

And the loudest laugh of all came from Willie's father!

* * *

The next day, Willie begged his mother for Gertie's bones.

"Whatever for?" she asked anxiously.

"I'm going to bury her come spring," he said.

"You don't want to do that, love. It's over and done with. It's best to forget."

"I don't want to forget. I want Gertie's bones."

His mother sighed and touched his cheek. Her son was changing, becoming more wilful day by day. "All right, wee Willie. If it's what you want, it's what you must have."

She cleaned the bones of meat and saved the grease in a jar to rub on wheezy chests. Then she placed the skeleton of Gertie, his dear feathered friend, into an empty boot box. She tied it with twine and handed it to Willie.

Reverently he carried it upstairs and placed it under the washstand beside his blue treasure chest. In the spring he would ask Alice to attend the funeral in the animal graveyard behind the barn. They had buried lots of little creatures there. He would ask her to say a few words over the grave. She was good with ceremonies, was Alice.

Then, and only then, would it be over and done with.

Chapter 11
Sad tidings

January passed uneventfully and, in spite of himself, Willie began to cheer up. Then, one bitter cold night, the Adams family was wakened by a rap, rap, rapping on the door.

Leaping from his warm bed, Henry Adams tugged at the window sash which was stuck fast with ice and snow. It flew open with a jolt and the biting wind wrapped around him like a chilly blanket.

"Who be ye?" he called down through the black night.

From the darkness below came a small, quavering voice. " 'Tis Joe . . . me mither's dead."

It was little Joe Long from down the road, sent by his father to bring the dreadful news. Emily Adams threw on her kimono and rushed down to open the door. The little boy crept gratefully inside. "Sit thyself down, little Joe," Mama said, "and I'll make thee a cup of cocoa to warm thy little insides."

So little Joe perched on the edge of the daybed

and tucked his mittenless hands between his trembling knees.

Willie stood uncertainly on the bottom step of the stairwell. Little Joe's awful message had set his flesh atremble.

I hope Papa never sends me in the night down the road, he thought with a shiver. I'd be feared, so I would. He looked at his mother bent over the stove, her long gold plait of hair glinting in the lamplight. "Don't die, Mama!" he whispered fiercely.

While Joe was supping his cocoa at the table, Mama lit a candle from the lamp and disappeared into the pantry alcove underneath the stairwell. Not knowing what to say to Joe, Willie followed her.

"What are you going to do, Mama?" he asked.

"Whatsoever I can, Willie."

Above their heads on a high shelf stood a row of jars filled with homemade remedies. "Too late it is for medicinals to help poor Sarah Long," murmured Mama, "but mayhap a drop of Grandma's favourite tonic will help soothe her husband's aching heart. Poor wee man, left alone to raise eight motherless children!"

Reaching for the bottle of ruby-red nectar, she removed the stopper and sniffed its contents. She nodded her head with satisfaction. The dark red fruit of the elder tree was good for many things: muffins and pies and pasties and puddings. But old

Grandma vowed it was best of all in Emily's famous tonic. Better by far than any doctor's foolish remedy. Why, just one sip and she felt stronger straightaway.

Little Joe had finished his cocoa and Mama had donned her coat and muffler. Papa had gone to hitch Dobbin to the cutter. Still Willie hadn't spoken to little Joe. Suddenly he knew what to do. Beside the stove, drying on the woodpile, were his new red mittens. "Here, Joe," he said, and he shoved them in the little boy's hands. "You can keep them if you like."

Little Joe, who had not spoken since he had said the awful words, managed a weak smile and murmured, "Thankee, Willie."

At the door Mama said to Nellie. "I'll depend on thee, daughter, to take care of things here."

"Don't worry about a thing, Mama," assured Nellie.

Then they were gone.

In the cold grey of the morning Artie and Alice and May took themselves off to school. Willie and Nellie were left alone with the old folks.

"First we'll do the barn chores," Nellie said, and they set off together down the frozen pathway.

Nellie did the milking and Willie fed the livestock, remembering to fill the horse's bin. Dobby will be hungry and thirsty whenever he gets home, he thought.

Just outside the barn door stood a wooden rain-barrel. It was full to the top and layered with a thick coat of ice. Standing on a block of wood, Willie cracked the ice with his father's axe. Then he hauled the icy water, bucket by bucket, until the trough was full to slopping over.

Back at the house old Grandpa had chopped the logs to fit the stove and piled the woodbox high. Old Grandma, in spite of her rheumatic fingers, had mended all the stockings and mittens. "Mama will be ever so pleased to find her basket empty," Nellie said, and the praise brought a smile to her grandmother's pain-lined face.

All the barn work had made Willie thirsty. But the fresh water pail was nearly empty, so he went down to the spring (which had never been known to freeze over) and hauled a pail of water up the hill.

"It's a fine help you've been this day, lad," Old Grandpa said as he helped himself to a dipperful of water.

"Then I'm not a layabout, am I, Grandpa?"

"No, indeed!" laughed the old man. "You're a better helper than most lads twice your age."

Sighing contentedly, Willie curled up on the daybed at old Grandma's feet. She tucked them under him for warmth.

Chapter 12
A great storm

I wonder if it's dark in the city yet? mused Willie. Mayhap the lamplighter is already making his way up Uncle Peter's street. Right this minute he might be torching the lamp on the lawn. His eyelids grew heavy with his imaginings, and he began to doze.

Suddenly his eyes popped open. He jumped up and went to the window to see how dark it was. But he couldn't see a thing through the thick white frost, so he began to make a peephole. Round and round his finger went until he had worn a hole the size of an English crown piece.

Willie knew how big an English crown was because old Grandpa had let him look inside his moneypouch one day. The old man had a small hoard of English money saved. Besides the crown there was a florin, two shillings, six farthings, and a tightly folded one pound note. Henry Adams grumbled that it was foolish waste, keeping English money about when it could just as easily be changed into good Canadian coin. But on this one point old

Grandpa stood firm. "If ever I hie away home to Nottingham," he said, "I'll need some ready cash in me pocket." And he had cautioned his grandson, "Thou art the only one who knows how much I've got in me hoard, Willie, so don't be tellin' anyone."

"I won't, Grandpa," promised Willie, pleased to be entrusted with the important secret.

Now Willie pressed his eye to the crown-size peephole in hopes of spying the cutter coming down the road. But all he saw was wildly swirling snow.

"It's darkening down, Nell," he worried. "I think a storm's coming on."

Suddenly, as if to prove him right, the wind howled down the chimney, making the stovepipes rattle furiously.

"I wish Mama and Papa were here," he said.

"They'll be along presently," assured his big sister, glancing at the clock, "I wish the children were safe home from school, that's what I wish."

"It's dreadfully blizzardy out there, Nell; mayhap they're lost."

"Don't say that, Willie!" She spoke so sharply that it made him jump. Then her voice softened. "Fetch more wood from the shed, there's a good lad, and I'll make some fresh cocoa to warm their little insides."

Nell sounds more like Mama every day, he thought as he hopped to do her bidding.

The storm grew steadily worse; the roaring wind, lashing the house, made a fearful wailing sound. In spite of the blazing fire in the stove, the kitchen grew ever colder.

Every few minutes Nellie came to look out Willie's peephole. Nothing but cyclones of snow! "Dear Lord," she prayed, "bring the children safely home."

"From thy lips to God's ear," murmured Grandpa.

No sooner had he said the words than the three came tumbling in the door. Bitter winds swirled in around them, chilling every corner of the kitchen.

"Eeee! Eeee! Eeee!" cried old Grandma, and old Grandpa piled on yet another blanket. (Ever since the onset of winter the old lady had been poorly. Oh, how she sorely longed for spring!)

Artie and Alice and May clapped their mittened hands and shook their clotted mufflers, and snowflakes went sailing through the air. Some landed on the hot stove, hissing and sizzling and vaporizing in little puffs of steam.

Willie wished he was a schoolboy. It must be ever so jolly to be lost in a blizzard and find your way home to hot cocoa steaming on the stove. Seven years old wasn't so grand after all. He wished he was eight or nine or ten.

"We had to bury our inkpots in the earth under the schoolhouse floor today, Nell," May said, warming her chillblained fingers around the hot cup.

"I remember doing that very thing when I was a schoolgirl," sighed the sixteen-year-old wistfully.

"Why must you bury your inkpots in the earth, May?" asked Willie curiously.

"So they don't freeze overnight on the tables," answered Artie shortly. "Anybody should know that."

"How can I know when I'm not allowed to go to school?" Willie grumbled.

"Mind your tongue!" snapped Artie.

Artie grows more like Papa every day, thought Willie crossly as he turned back to his peephole. Furry frost had filled it in again. So he circled round and round until his fingertip was numb.

Outside the wind had grown to gale-storm force. Inside the house grew dark and chill. May lit the largest lamp, Artie filled the woodbox once again, and old Grandpa fed the fire. Willie kept watch at the window. Alice drew up a chair beside her grandmother and began to rub her cold, bony hands. "I want me tea," murmured the poor old lady.

"It can't be tea time yet," protested Grandpa. "Wait a bit until our Emily comes."

But Nellie said, "I'll start the supper straightaway, Grandma." She was only too glad to have something to do to keep her mind from worry. She placed a large purple turnip on the chopping board and sliced it into rounds. After peeling the rounds, she chopped them into neat yellow squares and scooped them into the big iron kettle. Next she added a bowl of chicken stock, a pinch of salt, a scattering of parsley flakes, a minced onion, and a touch of sage. Lastly she dropped into the turnip soup an egg-sized dollop of fresh-churned butter.

"I hate turnips!" declared Willie.

"So do I, Willie," agreed Nell with a sigh. "But there's naught else left in the root cellar. Mama used up the last of the carrots and taties only yesterday."

Then Willie felt bad that he had criticized his sister's efforts. It wasn't her fault that there was naught else left but turnips. So when the pot began to simmer he gave an exaggerated sniff and said, "The soup smells good, Nell. I think I'm going to like it after all."

To stretch the meagre meal a little farther, Nellie fried up some bits of venison in porkfat drippings. When old Grandma tried to eat the crispy morsels she complained bitterly. " 'Tis tough as whalebone. 'Tis not fit fare for a toothless old body such as me."

After supper they all huddled round the stove.

Nellie opened the oven door to let the trapped heat out.

"When will they come, Nell?" whispered Alice.

"I want my mama!" cried May, her eyes brimming.

"Are they lost, Nell?" Artie put their worst fear into words. But Nellie didn't answer.

Willie sat shivering in the warm spot behind the stove. "They are lost aren't they, Nell?" he said.

"Pshaw, no!" she cried in as sure a tone as she could muster, "They'll be along any minute now."

"Mayhap Papa can't see through the blizzard," worried May between her sobs.

Closing his big leather-bound *History Of The Earth* book, old Grandpa peered over his eyeglasses. "Dobbin has no need to see," he reassured them. "He knows the road."

"Oh, Grandpa!" Nellie threw her arms gratefully around his stooped shoulders, "You know everything, you do."

Then she began to sing softly: "Papa's gone a hunting . . . Mama's grinding corn . . . And the children are all gathered . . . By the hearthside in the warm . . . "

"What's a hearthside, Nell?" puzzled Willie.

"An open fireplace, Willie."

"Uncle Peter's got a hearthside. I wish we had one."

"Be thankful for what you've got," grumbled Artie.

"I was only wishing," protested Willie.

"He was only wishing," repeated Alice.

"You leave our Willie alone," blubbered May.

"Mind your own business," growled Artie.

"Stop it! All of you! I can't stand your bickering." Even Nellie, who Mama always said was the soul of patience (and, indeed, her middle name was Patience), had finally lost her temper. So they all fell glumly silent.

It grew late. The lamplight guttered ominously. The grandfather clock struck seven but it could barely be heard above the storm.

Suddenly there was a thunderous, ear-splitting crash.

Nellie let out a piercing scream. Artie jumped about two feet in the air. May and Alice leapt into each others arms, Willie shook like a leaf, and old Grandpa dropped to his knees to comfort his weeping wife. Sam sprang yeowling from the woodpile to the table, missing the lamp by inches.

The old loghouse shuddered from floor to rafters. Old Grandma's china clinked and shattered in the sideboard. And a portrait of Queen Victoria fell right off the wall.

" 'Tis the end of the world! 'Tis the end of the

world!" cried Grandma in a voice amazingly strong for one so feeble.

"Don't be feared, Sophie," said Grandpa, holding tight to her hand. " 'Tis just a giant tree come down nearby. Thank God the house be spared."

But his words failed, this time, to comfort them.

Chapter 13
Safe and sound

Behind the stove in the warm spot, Willie sat hunched on the stool, his hands clamped over his ears, trying to be brave. Then he thought he heard something. A sound quite different from the storm. He unclasped his ears and listened harder. There it was again — a stomp, stomp, stomping.

Suddenly the door flew open and banged against the wall. And in blew Mama and Papa, covered in ice and snow. They stamped their feet and clapped their hands and clumps of snow fell from them in mounds upon the floor.

"Mama! Papa!" screamed the children. The gloom vanished like magic and everyone began talking at once.

"We heard a great tree fall, Mama."

"It made a dreadful noise and knocked Queen Victoria right off the wall."

"We weren't one bit afeared, Mama," piped up Willie.

"Of course you weren't, my brave soldiers,"

laughed Mama, mopping her wet face with the flannel.

"There's hot soup in the kettle," said Nellie.

"It smells mighty good to this wayfarer," said her father. Nellie beamed at his praise. (She was ever his favourite child, but he did not tell her so.)

"I'll dish it up for you, Papa," she offered.

"Later, daughter. First I must go to the barn." So saying, he lit the storm lantern and went directly out the woodshed door.

When old Grandpa could finally get a word in edgewise he asked, "How goes it with the Long family, Emily?"

"They be bearing up well, Puppa," she answered quietly.

Now the old pine kitchen seemed warm and cheerful again. Nellie ladled up for her mother a brimming bowl of steaming soup. Supping it gratefully to the last drop, Emily sighed, "Ahhh! 'Tis the best soup ever I tasted." Then she turned to her brood with a twinkle in her eye. "There's just one more task I'll have you do before it's time for bed."

"What is it, Mama?"

"Anything, Mama!"

"Tell us, tell us!"

Now that their parents were home again and they felt safe and sound, no job would seem too wearisome or hard.

"Come along then and follow me." She lit a candle from the lamp and led the way up the dark stairwell.

Away from the glowing stove, with the wind whistling about the window frames, the bedchambers were bitter cold. Snow sifted through the cracks in the chinking and frost was thick upon the iron bedstead posts.

" 'Tis ten below up here if I be any judge," said Emily, her breath forming little clouds in the air. " 'Tis frozen corpses we would be if we slept up here the night. So we'll just take up our beds . . . and walk!"

Whooping with delight, the children dragged and tumbled their mattresses and pillows down the stairs.

Shoving the table against the wall, they made room for their beds in the middle of the bare pine floor. Then Artie and Willie helped old Grandpa move the daybed (old Grandma and all) closer to the fire.

"Eeee! Eeee! Eeee!" cried the old lady, clutching the quilts under her bristly chin. "Don't thee dare dump me old bones upon the floor."

The children undressed hurriedly in the ice-cold parlour, first the girls, and then the boys. Jumping merrily into their makeshift pallets, the stuffing snapped and crackled like the breaking of a thousand tiny icicles. Soon the heat from the stove made the beds and the children warm and cosy.

Chapter 14
Storytime

When the kitchen at last quietened down, old Grandma glanced at the clock. "Henry's gone overlong at the barn," she observed.

With a pang of remorse Emily realized how the time had flown. Quickly she reached for her damp coat and muffler. But her father stopped her. "It's my place to go, Emily," he said, and began pulling on his boots. Then he tucked his long grey hair under his cap and his daughter was just helping him on with his overcoat when the woodshed door crashed open and Henry came staggering through it, half blinded by the blizzard, his brown beard and moustache bushy-white with frost.

"So much running in and out," moaned old Grandma. " 'Tis enough to freeze me marrow."

"I'll warm a fieldstone for you, Grandma," said Alice. Under the stove were several smooth flat stones. She popped one into the oven, and when it was hot, wrapped it in a thick flannel and tucked it at her grandmother's cold and bony feet.

Henry Adams did not speak, nor did anyone

question him, until he was dry and snug and supping his hot turnip soup.

"What kept thee so long, Henry?" asked his wife.

"I was trapped inside by a bear," he replied.

"A bear! A bear!" cried Willie gleefully. "Tell us all about it, Papa."

"Not much to tell," said Papa. "There he stood on his hind legs at the barn door, him wanting in and me wanting out. Bye! I wish I'd taken me gun! Any-the-way, I waited him out and he finally trundled off."

"Surely he meant thee no harm, Papa," said Willie. "Only cold he was, and needing shelter."

"What would a bear be doing out of his den on a night such as this?" puzzled old Grandpa.

"Aye," agreed old Grandma, " 'tis not a fit night for man nor beast."

At her mother's words, Emily got a faraway look in her eyes. Her children, seeing that look, knew a story was coming.

"Do you mind the time, Muma," began Emily, "when Puppa and Peter were snowbound in town and thee and me and baby James were all alone in the house?"

"Oh, aye, I mind . . . " Old Grandma's faded eyes suddenly grew brighter, "T'was just such a night as this is."

Snuggling under the quilts, the children waited breathlessly. There was nothing they liked better to hear than their elders' tales of long ago.

"I was just a wee bit girl at the time," mused Emily.

"Oh, wee'er by far than Willie," interrupted her mother, pulling herself up into a half-sitting position. "I remember as if t'was yesterday. I had gone off to the barn to tend the animals, just as Henry did the night, leaving thee to care for baby James." She sighed and sank back on her pillows.

"Aye," Emily picked up the thread of the story. "The loghouse was filled with eerie sounds and the candles gave such a wee bit light and cast such frightful shadows. We had no lovely oil lamps to lighten up the dark corners in those days." She turned up the lamp's wick and the flame grew brighter. "Well, baby James began to cry so I dipped a rag-sucket into the treacle pail and held it to his mouth. He stopped crying then, and in the sudden quiet I heard an odd scratching at the window." Ten glistening eyes followed her pointing finger to the window. "I glanced up, all unsuspecting, and there, staring right in at me, were the crazed yellow eyes of a wolf, with his long red tongue lolling out."

"Oh, Mama, what did you do?" gasped May, as fearful as if she'd never heard the tale before.

"So frightened was I that I threw the sucket

into the air and baby James began to scream, so I gave the cradle such a hard rock that he flew right out on the floor."

"Then what happened, Mama?" whispered Nellie.

"I scooped up my poor little brother as best I could and tucked him back into the cradle. And off to sleep he went, frightened out of his wits, poor lamb."

"Then did you have to go and save Grandma?" asked Artie, forgetting that his mother was only a wee bit girl at the time.

"No, indeed. Your grandma had to save me."

"What did you do, Grandma?" asked Alice.

"Do!" The old woman raised herself up and cackled at the memory. "Why, I slew a chicken with the axe and flang it out the barn door; the blood splattered like red berries in the snow. Then the wolf made for the chicken and I flew like the wind to the house."

Now the two women looked at each other, the memory bright between them. "She was a brave wee person, was your Grandma," said Emily as her mother sank back on the pillows.

Oh, it was lovely . . . warm on the floor . . . the fire roaring . . . the winds howling . . . and Mama and Grandma storytelling.

Then Artie, not wanting storytime to end, said,

"Tell us about the night you had your vision, Grandma."

"Oh, aye, me vision . . . " The old lady's eyes glittered in the lamplight . . . "As large as life it was, and as true as we're all gathered here. I woke from a sound sleep in the middle of the night and sat bolt upright in bed. And there she was, me sister, Polly, who I hadn't set eyes upon for nigh on twenty years. Now I knew she was across the sea in England, yet there she stood inside me bedchamber right here in the loghouse."

"Was she a ghost, Grandma?" whispered May.

"No, lass, she was as real as me and thee. Though I have no proof, because your Grandpa, foolish man, slept right through it. 'Is that you, Polly?' I asked. And plain as I'm speaking to you she says, 'Aye, Sophie, 'tis me. I've come to say farewell.' Then she pointed with a pale finger at the washstand. 'Look at the timepiece,' she says. So I picked up thy grandpa's pocketwatch and I saw in the eerie light that it was two o'clock in the mornin'. 'Goodbye, Sophie . . . God bless . . . 'til we meet again.' Then, pouff, she was gone right before mine eyes."

The children knew there was more to come, but old Grandma seemed about to fall asleep in the middle of the story. So Alice shook her hand gently and begged, "Tell us the rest, Grandma."

The tired old eyes flicked open. "Well, no one

believed me, not even thy Grandpa, and he was a believing man. So I moped about for weeks, me nerves frayed and frazzled, and then it came . . . the letter edged in black. It was from me sister's husband, Wortley. He wrote that Polly had departed this life on the very night and at the very moment of me visitation."

"Don't be daft, woman!" interrupted Papa crossly. "Visions are stuff and nonsense. It doesn't do to stir up old memories. It'll give the children nightmares."

Then Mama spoke quietly, "Mine own dear Grandmama used to say 'God gave us memory . . . that we might have roses in December!' "

"Such memories will grow weeds instead of roses," grunted Papa. So saying, he blew out the lamp. Then he and Mama drew woolen shawls about their shoulders and settled back in their chairs, prepared to sit up all the night long to keep the stove alight.

The fire glowed red through the little draught door. The logs shifted and crackled cosily. Old Grandpa, wrapped in a blanket, began to snore from the rocker. Old Grandma's breathing came soft and shallow from the couch. And one by one the children fell asleep.

Chapter 15
Digging out time

Five days and nights the tempest raged. The log-house was snowed in by a solid white wall. The lamps were lit both day and night, and only the grandfather clock in the corner told the difference.

Since the storm began no one, not even Henry, had been able to get to the spring.

" 'Tis lucky we are to have clean fresh snow for water," remarked Mama as she chopped a pailful right out of the kitchen doorway. "Straight from heaven it comes, just like manna in the good book."

"Aye." Papa's brow was furrowed. "But how shall I get to the barn?" He feared for his animals. Four days the poor creatures had not been tended.

On the sixth day the family woke to a strange new sound.

Silence.

"What is it, Mama?" Willie looked up from the mattress on the floor.

"The storm has passed," answered his mother.

"It's digging out time," added his father.

"Whew! It's dreadful hot in here." Artie threw back the covers.

"The temperature must be up by thirty degrees," agreed Papa.

Just then·there came a mysterious sound from above. Plain as day they heard it. Footsteps . . . on the roof!

"It's the bear! It's the bear!" cried Willie, bouncing with glee on the mattress.

"Hush!" Mama pressed a finger to her lips. The whole family stayed as still as statues, save Papa, who loaded his gun. "Oh, Papa," pleaded Willie, "please don't shoot him."

"Hold your tongue!" hissed his father.

Clump, clump, clump went the footsteps on the roof. Then down the chimney and through the stovepipe they heard a ghostly voice, "Henry Adams! Henry Adams!"

Mama gasped, the old folks clung together, and the children, all except Willie, dove under the covers. And even Henry Adams looked a mite dismayed.

"Henry Adams . . . are ye in there?" The voice came clearer now.

Lifting the stove lid, Papa shouted right into the fire, "Aye, I am. Who be ye?"

" 'Tis me, Tom Rome. Can ye let me in?"

Tom Rome and his brother Elgin were bachelors who lived in a one-room cabin some distance to the north.

Papa and Mama hurried up the stairs to let Tom in through the bedchamber window, which was the only opening left to the outside world. He had snowshoed all the way, he said, walking right over fences and even clearing the tops of trees at times.

" 'Tis me brother, Elgin," he explained. "You'll be hard put to believe what happened."

"Tell us then," urged Mama.

"It was the night of the great storm. He'd been over to the Danders' place sparkin' Sarah-Jane." Tom winked and grinned and Papa growled, "Get on with it."

"I warned him not to go," continued Tom, frowning now to make up for the wink. "But he said he'd be fine in his bearskin coat. Well, it was that very coat that was his undoing. On his way home the blizzard grew so fierce that Elgin got down on all fours to cross the meadow. And at that very moment Joshua Porter was passing by in his cutter. He saw what he thought was a black bear making for our cabin so he took aim with his rifle and fired. He hit Elgin hard in the side and he's bleeding bad, Mrs. Adams."

He didn't need to say any more. Emily quickly prepared her medicine bag and bundled up warm. Her husband fastened snowshoes on her feet securely. Then out she went with their neighbour, through the window into the bright sunlight.

"You'll take care now!" called Papa after Mama. And she gave a backward wave to reassure him.

It was more than a mile trek to Tom and Elgin's cabin. By snowshoe it was a long hard way to go.

Mama returned that night, ever so tired but ever so pleased with herself. "The wound was clean and no vital organ had been scathed," she explained. "I was able to dig the bullet out and purify the hole. So Elgin Rome will live to tell the tale of the fearful night when Joshua Porter mistook him for a bear."

After catching her second wind she asked, "How did the livestock fare, Henry?"

"Better than expected," answered her husband. After dragging the bedding back up the stairs, Artie and Willie had worked all day helping him dig a tunnel to the barn. "Snow aplenty blew through the cracks, so they didn't lack for water. The feedbins were all empty but me and the boys filled them up. The animals should be right as rain tomorrow."

Later, as Emily dragged her weary feet up the creaking staircase the children heard her say, " 'Tis lucky we are to have so many blessings to count. But I cannot count them tonight, husband."

"The morrow will be soon enough, wife," their father answered. And then they heard him laugh.

Chapter 16
An early spring

As if to make up for the terrible winter, mother nature brought on an early spring.

One bright blue sunny morning, Willie came down the stairs rubbing the sleep from his eyes.

"Good morning to you, sleepyhead," said Mama. Then she added, "There's something to see under the stove."

Curiously Willie got down on his hands and knees to look. There, curled up on her side on a bed of rags, was Samantha. And snuggled up to her soft grey stomach were four mewling blind kittens.

"Oh, Sam! Sam!" Willie cried happily. "It's a mama you are!" Gently he stroked the hump of her back and she blinked at him with proud emerald eyes.

All morning long Mama let him sit and watch the kittens. And Papa said nothing when he forgot to do his chores.

Then in the afternoon, on his way back up the path from the outhouse, he caught sight of Artie standing off in the brushwood. His brother was leaning over a washtub with a long stick in his hand.

"What are you doing, Artie?" called Willie.

"None of your business!" retorted the older boy.

But Willie was inquisitive, so he started through the brushwood.

"If you come one step closer I'll throw you away by the lugs!" threatened Artie.

But Willie knew that Artie didn't dare to do that anymore, so he walked right up to the washtub.

"Get away! Get away!" yelled his brother.

Yet Willie couldn't stop himself from peering down into the tub of snowy water. Artie was holding a lumpy potato sack underwater with a stick. The sack squirmed and wriggled and a steady stream of bubbles rose to the surface.

"What is it, Artie?" Fear clutched at his heart. "What are you doing?"

Suddenly his brother gave him a hard shove that sent him sprawling into a snowdrift.

Then Willie knew.

Scrambling to his feet, he ran screaming into the house. "Mama! Mama! Where are Sam's kittens?"

Dropping the cooking spoon with a splatter, she reached out and gathered him into her arms. "I'm sorry, little one," she said, "but they had to be put to sleep."

Wrenching free from her embrace he yelled accusingly, "But . . . but . . . they're not being put to sleep. They're being drowned, Mama, *drowned*."

"It's the only thing to do, hinny." She spread her hands helplessly. "Two barn cats and a housecat is all we'll ever need."

But Willie cried, "We could give them over to Maudie. She loves cats. And we could ask the Hicklings and the Danders and the Longs do they want a kitten."

"They all have more than enough," his mother explained.

He knew, then, that it was too late to save Sam's kittens. So he sat himself down on the stool behind the stove and watched the grey cat as she prowled mournfully about the kitchen looking for her children. Once he tried to take her up on his lap but she leapt away, refusing to be comforted.

"Artie is bad, Mama," declared Willie.

"No, Willie, he is only doing thy father's bidding."

"Then Papa is bad." He dared to say this without so much as a glance around to see who might be listening.

"No, hinny. Thy papa is strict, to be sure, but bad he is not. He always tries to do what's best."

Willie scrubbed at his eyes. "We could have set them loose in the forest and they would have turned into bobcats."

"Bobcat's prey, more like it, Willie. Or dinner for a hawk. No, 'tis kinder to drown newborn kittens. They don't suffer that way."

"Sam is suffering," Willie said as she continued sniffing and crying into dark corners.

"Aye, poor little mother." Mama came over and cupped his chin in her hand. "I'm sorry it makes thee sad, love."

He twisted his chin away. "I'm more nor sad, Mama."

Willie ate no supper that night, and no one asked him why.

After dark he went down the path and around the back to the far side of the barn. The moon was full and bright. He could see as plain as day the fresh mound of dirt and snow piled up on the soggy ground. He knew Sam's kittens were buried there in the animal graveyard. But he didn't have the heart to sing "God Save The Queen" over them. Tears ran down his face and glistened like dewdrops in the starlight. He thought that he would never feel so sorrowful again.

But he was soon to learn the meaning of one of old Grandma's favourite sayings — that trouble always comes in pairs.

Chapter 17
Two pennies

Ever after the great storm (in later years it came to be known as the Great Storm of '89) old Grandma grew steadily weaker. For some time now, the parlour had been turned into a sickroom so that Emily could nurse her mother without running up and down the stairs.

One rainy April morning she came out of the parlour and softly closed the door. Her eyes bright with tears, she went straight to her father's side. Putting a gentle arm around his sagging shoulders, she whispered, "Puppa, Muma's gone."

At first Willie didn't know what his mother meant. Gone! Gone where? Why, for the past few weeks old Grandma couldn't even sit up, let alone get up and go.

But when Papa shouldered his spade and went to the churchyard, taking Artie with him, then he knew. Old Grandma was dead . . . like Sam's kittens.

While her husband and son were gone, Emily

Adams prepared her mother for everlasting sleep. She bathed the fragile, wasted frame and plaited the wispy hair. She dressed her in her Sunday frock and folded her small parchment hands over her shallow breast. Finally she placed two pennies on the sunken eyelids.

So lost was Emily in thought that she failed to notice Willie standing in the doorway. "Why are you doing that, Mama?" he asked wonderingly, pointing to the pennies.

"To make sure her eyes stay quite shut," she answered truthfully. "I'll remove them bye and bye."

Nellie and May had hitched Dobbin to the buggy and set out to spread the news. Alice had stayed home to help her mother. It was her sad task to sew the black mourning bands on all their clothes.

"Be sure to sew them on the left sleeves by the heart, love," Mama said.

"Yes, Mama," said Alice.

The bands on the children's clothes were one inch wide. The adults wore two-inch bands. With tears running down her cheeks, Alice sewed the almost invisible stitches. She was a fine needle-woman, was Alice.

Meantime, Willie went to old Grandpa and, big as he was, climbed up on his grandfather's lap and rested his head on his chest. Tears spilled down the old man's cheeks and trickled onto Willie's head.

"Don't cry, Grandpa," whispered Willie. "You've still got me."

"Ah, laddie . . . " The grandfather tightened his arm around the boy and drew him closer. "What would I do without thee to comfort me?"

Uncle Peter and Uncle James arrived the next day, but Auntie Meg couldn't come because little Emily had whooping cough. Willie was sorely disappointed. He had been looking forward to seeing his tiny cousin again.

Mama's two brothers helped Papa carry old Grandma's coffin from the barn into the parlour. (It was the custom in those days to make the plain pine box before ever it was needed. Old Grandpa's box was out there, too, stored high out of sight in the rafters.)

The funeral took place on the fourth day. The good country folk came for miles around, laden with food and sympathy. Reverend Mackenzie rode in on horseback all the way from Huntsville. During the eulogy he told the grieving family that they must not feel sad, because such a fine old lady as Grandma would most certainly go straightaway to heaven.

This news cheered Willie right up and he stopped crying. After all, he reasoned, old Grandma had been laid up with the miseries for many years now. And Reverend Mackenzie said that she would be cured the minute she set foot in heaven. She would be ever so much happier, Willie thought, flying about free as a bird in heaven instead of lying ailing on the daybed in the kitchen. And besides, she would meet her sister, Polly, there and they would have a fine time catching up on each other's news.

From where he sat on the horsehair sofa between Mama and Papa, Willie could see old Grandma's pale profile etched against the dark-stained wood. Her small grey head rested on a satin pillow, the softest pillow ever she slept on, he thought. Her skin was the colour of tallow, but the wrinkles had all but disappeared, as if someone had smoothed them out with a flatiron. He'd never seen old Grandma look so comfortable and peaceful before. Mayhap she's there already, he thought hopefully.

They buried her in the churchyard alongside her own dead "childring." (Twin babies, brother and sister to Emily and Peter and James, had died of the ague many long years ago.) When the committal ceremony was over, Papa and the uncles stayed behind to shovel in the dirt.

The women of Elderberry had spread a lovely feast upon the table. Indeed, it was the most food anyone had seen since the last funeral repast. Each woman had brought the best she had left in her nearly empty larder. There were roasted rabbits, two boiling hens, pickled pig's feet, a roll of stuffed venison, three loaves of freshly baked bread and a platter piled high with potato cakes. For dessert Maudie Hanley had brought her last two sealers of wild strawberry preserves and a batch of sourdough biscuits.

Reverend Mackenzie licked his lips, clasped his hands, and said a hasty blessing. Then they all dug in.

The Adams' children ate hungrily. But there was one particular offering that they all politely refused. It was Mrs. Joseph Hickling's golden brown turnip loaf.

"You will eat a slice," their father told them sternly, "or you will march to the barn and do the chores."

So off they trooped, all five of them, to the barn.

Chapter 18
Let's ride Dobby!

"I forgot to spit on my wart this morning," remarked Willie, examining the seedy bump on his middle finger.

"If you forget even once it takes a week of morning spittle to make up," said Alice knowingly.

They were sitting on old Grandma's stone in the churchyard, soaking up the warm June sunshine. They had finished tidying the plot, like Mama had said, and were having a little rest.

It was old Grandma herself who had taught them how to get rid of their warts. "When I was a wee girlie, back home in Nottingham," she used to say, "me hands were fairly covered in warties. T'was mine own dear Grandmama who told me that spittle in the morning was filled with magic medicine. And so it was! In just a fortnight's time me warties had vanished. All twenty-seven of them."

Mama said it was just an old wives' tale, and a nasty thing to do. Only milk from the milkweed pod was a proper cure for warts, she insisted. But her children liked old Grandma's remedy better, and they could be heard spitting on their warts before even the sun was up. Then, in just a few short days, the little growths began to shrivel and disappear. So their mother had to admit that perhaps morning spittle was a magic potion after all.

Willie pressed his black-stockinged legs flat against the warmth of the homemade marker and looked up at the clear blue sky. He could tell by the position of the sun that it was still morning, so he rolled the saliva around in his mouth until it was full, then spat upon the wart as hard as ever he could.

"That won't do," insisted Alice. "The magic's gone the minute you wipe your teeth with the flannel."

She was sitting beside him, her eyes closed, her long brown hair sweeping the stone behind her.

"I'm hungry," complained Willie. "I wish the carrots and beans were up in Mama's garden."

"They'll be up soon," assured his sister. "If we don't get another frost. Any-the-way, the turnips are finally gone, thank goodness."

"Thank goodness," echoed Willie. "When I grow up I'm never going to eat turnips. I'm going to live in the city where turnips don't even grow."

"Me, too, Willie. I'm going to be a nurse you know."

"I'm going to be a lamplighter."

"I know."

"Why don't you be a doctor, Alice?"

"I don't think they let ladies be doctors, Willie."

"Who are 'they'?"

Alice puckered her brow. "Sir John A. MacDonald, I guess. He's Prime Minister. Or maybe it's Queen Victoria. But you wouldn't think the Queen would object, being a lady herself."

"Well, I heard old Grandpa read out loud from the *Journal* that a lady doctor in New York did an operation and saved a man's life and everything."

"Really, Willie?" Alice was all ears. "Oh, wouldn't that be grand. Then I could take care of all our family and Papa wouldn't have to worry about doctor bills anymore."

"I'm hungry," Willie said again.

"Well, let's see if there are some wild strawberries on the hill," suggested Alice.

They both jumped up and climbed over the fence stile that separated the graveyard from the meadow. Not far away Bessie, and Dobbin were grazing side by side.

"Hello there, Bessie!" Willie rubbed between her horns. "Is the fresh grass good after that dusty old hay?" She answered in a soft, lowing moo. Then he bent down to where Dobbin was munching the tender green shoots. Only yesterday Willie had heard Papa say Dobbin was getting a bit long in the tooth. So Willie pushed back his velvety muzzle to see.

"You do have long teeth, Dobby," he agreed.

Alice had plodded on ahead, so Willie hurried to catch up to her, the soft spring mud sucking at his boots.

"There's nary a flower, never mind a berry," she told him, fingering the baby plants nestled on the hillside. "So let's go home, Willie, and see what Mama's got cooking in the pot."

"I'm too tired to walk that far yonder," moaned Willie, shielding his eyes as he gazed across the meadow. The loghouse seemed a far piece away. Suddenly Willie's eyes lit up. "Let's ride home on Dobby!" he cried.

Alice frowned at the suggestion. "What would Papa say?"

But Willie begged, "Please, Ally, please!"

"Oh, all right then . . . give a whistle."

Willie whistled and the horse came galloping towards them, stopping in a splatter of mud and grass. With his hands he made a foothold and boosted his sister up. Then she reached down and hoisted him up behind her.

"Giddy-up, Dobby, giddy-up," cried Willie, and away flew the good old workhorse across the field towards home.

Alice clung with both fists to his tossing mane. Willie clung for dear life to Alice.

Oh, it was grand to fly with Dobby over the greening meadow at breathless, bounding speed. Then, as sudden as a bolt of lightning, the horse's right hoof plunged into a groundhog hole, sending his heavy body crashing to the ground.

And away flew Willie and Alice, sailing through the air!

Alice lay stunned for a moment; she sat up slowly and felt the lump that was rising on her head. Through blurry hazel eyes she saw Dobbin struggling to his feet. He gave his head a good shake, whinnied his disapproval, and went galloping off to join Bessie.

Thank the dear Lord Dobby's not hurt, was the first thought that came to Alice. She knew her father would never forgive them if any harm came to his workhorse.

But Willie! Where was her little brother? Leaping to her feet, heedless of the pain that went flashing through her forehead, she screamed, "Willie! Willie! *Willie!*"

There was no answer so she began to search. She found him sprawled behind a big grey boulder.

His eyes were closed and his face was sheet-white. His right leg was twisted strangely, and blood gushed through the torn black stocking of the left one.

"Oh, wee Willie!" sobbed Alice, gathering him into her arms. She knew she must get him home. But how? The loghouse was too far away for her to carry him. So she gently lowered him back onto the grass, tore the hem from her soiled petticoat, and bound up the bleeding leg.

"I'll run for help, Willie," she told the senseless boy, "Don't you fret, now. Mama will know what to do."

Then she gathered her muddy skirts above her knees and raced like the wind towards home.

Chapter 19
Courage!

In the loghouse all was peaceful until Alice came stumbling in the door. At first she just stood there, panting and bedraggled, shaking from head to toe.

Her mother looked up and dropped the cooking spoon into the pot, splashing broth hither and thither. "What is it, child? What's happened?"

"It's . . . it's . . . it's . . . " Alice darted a glance at her father and couldn't go on.

"Speak, child, speak!" urged her mother.

"It's wee Willie. He's hurt ever so bad. I couldn't carry him so I left him in the pasture by the big rock."

Mama gasped and Papa looked up from the washbasin. "How did it happen?" he asked.

As Alice told him in a quavering voice, his bearded face hardened. Quickly he dried his hands on the flannel. "What about me horse?" he demanded.

"Oh, Dobbin's fine, Papa. It's only Willie who's hurt."

He turned his back on her then and spoke to his eldest son, "You, Arthur, come with me."

At the door, Nellie plucked at his sleeve. "Don't be vexed, Papa," she whispered. "Only pray that our Willie is safe."

Seeing the anxiety in the eyes of his favourite child, his expression softened. "Aye," he said. "We'll fetch him home, never fear."

When Papa and Artie were gone, May and Nellie cleared the big board table and Mama covered it with a clean white sheet.

* * *

The pain when they moved him was ever so bad. Willie had to bite his lip so as not to cry out loud. His father and brother entwined their hands to make a seat and carried him gently home. Carefully they laid him on the table.

Then his mother began, cautiously, to strip his stockings off and wash away the dirt and blood. As she worked she murmured soothingly, "Have no fear, little one, thy mama has thee now."

When the wound was clean she saw that a gaping hole lay bare the bone in Willie's left leg. " 'Tis lucky we are the artery has gone unscathed," she said. Then with needle and thread, boiled clean for the purpose, she stitched the jagged wound. The leg was so numb Willie felt no pain at all as the needle went in and out. Soon the tear was mended.

The other leg was a different matter. "We'll be needing Doctor Stokes, Henry. This is more than I can reckon with." Without a backward glance Henry Adams set off for Huntsville.

Then old Grandpa came out of the pantry with a bottle of old Grandma's favourite remedy. "Have a sup of this, lad," he said kindly. "It'll ease thy pain."

When Willie was finally settled down Mama turned to Alice. "Oh, my dear!" Her hand flew to her throat at the sight of the huge purple lump on her daughter's forehead. "Forgive thy thoughtless mama." Immediately she made a flannel pad and soaked it in cold water from the spring. Then Nellie and May helped their sister up to bed, holding the compress to her head and with strict orders from Mama not to let her fall asleep.

When Dr. Stokes arrived, Willie's ordeal was not so bad, because his mother sprinkled chloroform on a handkerchief and held it to his nose while the doctor worked. The smell was nasty but it sent him off to sleep.

When he woke he found himself cosy and clean on the daybed with his mother standing by. "Well, now, look who's come back to the land of the livin'!" she declared. "Would you like a wee bit of broth to help mend thy broken leg?"

"Yes, Mama. I'm ever so hungry," he said. But when he tried to sit up something tugged at his leg, making him cry out in pain. Looking down, he saw that his leg was bound between two wooden slats, and under his foot, dangling over the edge of the daybed, was an iron bar in a sling.

"What's that for?" he cried in alarm.

"Don't worry," Mama said. "It's a weight to stretch your leg so that when it's healed it won't be shorter than the other."

"How long will it hang there?"

"Oh, just a little while I think," answered his mother. Then she began spooning in the steaming broth to take his mind away.

Two weeks later Emily deftly snipped the stitches in his left leg and they came out clean as a whistle, leaving a long red scar. Willie was ever so proud of his scar.

But two whole months went by before Doctor Stokes removed the weight and splints, and in all that time the pain never ceased, except when old Grandpa gave him a sup of Grandma's medicine, or Doctor Stokes insisted that he take a sleeping potion.

When he finally stood on his own two feet again he found that he was weak and wobbly. So he clung to the arm of old Grandpa's rocker for support and Grandpa steadied him.

Then his father said, "Come along, boy, show a little grit. Do you want to be a lifelong layabout?"

The harsh words filled him with determination. He let go of the rocker, took one cautious step, and then another, until he stood right in front of his father. "There, I did it!" he declared triumphantly.

"You did indeed," his father said, and the smile on his lips made Willie feel that at last his father had come to like him better.

Now Willie turned towards the doctor. "Thank you for fixing my leg, Doctor Stokes," he said. "It feels almost as good as new."

The medical man smiled, then answered solemnly, "It wasn't just my doing, Willie. If you hadn't borne the suffering like a man and I had had to loosen the weight even a fraction, you might have spent the rest of your life hobbling about with one leg shorter than the other."

"Aye, he's a brave lad, me grandson," said old Grandpa proudly.

And finally Willie went to his mother. "Thank you for my special scar, Mama. It looks just like a railroad track."

She reached out and hugged him and Willie hugged her back as hard as ever he could.

Chapter 20
A dream?

The loghouse was pitch dark when little Willie woke. At first he could not imagine what had wakened him. Then he heard the muffled voices of his parents drifting up from the kitchen below. He strained his ears towards the bare pine floor but could not make out what they were saying.

Then the strangest feeling came over him . . . as if all this had happened before. It was just like reading a storybook for the second time. You knew exactly what was coming next, but you were excited anyway.

Sure enough, a candle flickered in the dark hallway, casting weird shadows on the wall. Then his mother poked her head around the doorjamb and beckoned him to follow.

The grandfather clock in the kitchen struck four. Sam came out from under the hot stove yawning and stretching. She began to sharpen her claws on the old pine table leg. "Scat!" hissed Papa, and Willie gathered the cat onto his lap.

After breakfast Papa went out with the lantern to hitch Dobbin to the buggy. Willie washed up, not forgetting behind his ears. Then he began to dress in his Sunday-go-meeting suit. That's when he noticed that something *was* different. The suit was much too small, so he must have grown! And today it wasn't raining. The golden sun came blazing over the treetops. The forest sparkled like diamonds with early morning dew.

The fine weather made old Dobbin frisky. He trotted along at a steady clip, bringing them early to the wayside station. And this time Willie was allowed to help his father flag down the Northern as it came whistling out of the wilderness.

"Well, boy . . . " Papa said in his usual gruff manner, "behave yourself, and take care of your mother."

"Yes, Papa, I will. But, Papa . . . "

The train had come to a full stop, huffing and chuffing and billowing steam. *"What is it, boy?"* Henry Adams hollered over the noise of the engine.

Willie steeled himself and looked straight into his father's eyes. *"Don't call me 'boy' any-the-more!"* he hollered back. Then he scrambled up the high iron steps after his mother.

The conductor called *"ALLLABOOARD!"* and clanged the half-gate shut. The train began to move, leaving Henry Adams with a perplexed expression on his face. Then, just before they lost sight of each other their eyes met. Suddenly Henry's arm shot up and, waving wildly, he shouted at the top of his lungs, *"GOODBYE, WILLIAM!"*

"GOODBYE, PAPA!" cried Willie as loud as ever he could.

Then he and Mama found themselves a seat, the very same seat as last time, it seemed to Willie, and settled down for their long journey.

Was this really happening or was it a dream? Willie decided to pinch himself to find out. "Ouch!" he yelped.

"What's the matter, hinny?" asked his mother anxiously.

"Nothing, Mama," laughed Willie. "I was just pinching myself to see if I was dreaming."

His mother smiled and said, "No, 'tis not a dream, lad. We're off and away again, just me and thee."

"Why are we going this time, Mama?"

"The reason's the same as before."

"Auntie Meg is going to have a baby?"

"Aye."

"But, why, Mama, when she's already got Emily?"

"Well, hinny, wee Emily needs a brother or sister to keep her company. Just think how lonely you would be without your sisters and brother."

Willie sat back and thought about it. He knew he liked having sisters . . . but he wasn't so sure about his brother.

Once again the singing of the rails sent him off to sleep and the next thing he knew the train was pulling into Parkdale Station in Toronto. And there was Uncle Peter pacing the platform just like last year.

Taking his sister's grip from her hand, he kissed her on the cheek. Then he offered his hand to his nephew. Willie took it uncertainly. No one had ever shaken his hand before.

"Well, young man," — not "nipper" or "boy," but young man! Uncle Peter must have noticed how much he'd grown! — "and how's the broken leg? Right as rain, I hope."

"Fine, thank you. Right as rain," agreed Willie, strutting along beside his uncle to prove how fine it was.

When they arrived at Uncle Peter's house Mama went straight upstairs, just like last year. But this time Willie didn't have to sit in the parlour. Instead he was led into the big bright kitchen to play with Emily.

Oh, how he liked her! She was ever so beautiful. And her head (which was much bigger than his Christmas orange now) was covered in chestnut curls.

Uncle Peter said Emily's favourite game was peek-a-boo. So Willie peek-a-booed for hours and never got tired of the baby's tinkling laughter.

When tea time came Mama did not come downstairs. Instead, Mrs. Murphy came in from next door. In the city your neighbour's house was only steps away.

She set right to work making supper, and when she wanted to brew the tea she filled the kettle from a water pump right at the kitchen sink. Imagine! A water pump right at the kitchen sink. Imagine! A water pump right inside your house!

"It's a miracle," marvelled Willie. "When I grow up I'm going to have a house like this." He had made up his mind for certain. Much as he loved the loghouse in Muskoka still, the city was the place for him, what with indoor water pumps and feather beds and gas jets and streetlamps.

Streetlamps!

After supper, when Emily had been put to bed, Uncle Peter gave Willie permission to sit on the veranda swing.

The sun had just dropped behind the houses on the other side of the street. He waited, swinging impatiently, last year's memories rushing over him.

When it was quite dark he leaned far out over the railing and stared down the cedar-block road. There it was — the bobbing light, at the very end of the street! Slowly it made its way towards him. At last it stopped in front of Uncle Peter's house. When the lamp was lit the lamplighter thrust the pole into the turf, just like last year, and mopped his sweating brow. Then Willie jumped up from the swing and leapt down the veranda steps from top to bottom. "Good evening to you, sir!" he cried breathlessly.

"Well, good evening to you lad. Back again, I see."

He remembered! The lamplighter remembered him! That gave Willie the courage to ask something he was longing to know. "Could you tell me, sir," he said, trying to sound very grown-up, "how old a man must be to learn your occupation?" (It's lucky he was that May had taught him such a fine big word.)

"Well, now let me see . . . " The lamplighter scratched his head to help him think. "I do believe our youngest apprentice has just gone fourteen years."

"Oh, my . . . " Willie tried to hide his disappointment. "It's a long time I'll have to wait to be a lamplighter. But that's what I'm going to be when I grow up."

"Are you now?" The man was plainly pleased. "Well, when you're ready for the job, be sure to say that Michael Flanagan recommends ye." So saying, he continued on his way, the gas lights glowing in his wake.

"Thank you, Mr. Flanagan!" called Willie after him.

Oh, just wait 'til I tell Artie! thought Willie jubilantly. Mr. Flanagan recommends me!

After breakfast the next morning his mother took him up the carpeted stairs to see Auntie Meg and her new baby. This time it was a boy.

The first thing his aunt said when she saw him was, "Why, wee Willie, how you've grown!" Then it must be true! He could hardly wait for his birthday so that his mother would measure him against the wall. Mayhap he was even big enough to go to school at last.

Willie kissed Auntie Meg on the cheek, then he peeked into the cradle.

"Can you guess his name?" she asked.

"Peter, perhaps, because Uncle Peter is his papa?"

"That's a good guess, and indeed his middle name is Peter. But his first name is William, after you Willie. What do you think of that?"

Willie was overcome by the honour. Imagine being not quite eight years old and already having someone named for you. "I think it's grand!" he exclaimed, then added loyally, "But Emily will always be my favourite cousin."

Auntie Meg smiled and closed her eyes. Then he and his mother tiptoed out across the soft floral matting that covered the bedchamber floor.

*   *   *

On the journey home in the train, Willie was unusually quiet. He was thinking very deeply. More than ever this year he had noticed the grandness of Uncle Peter's house. The wonderful water pump. The blue gas jets in the parlour. The carpeted floors. The shiny tables. The lace counterpanes. And the feather mattress he had been allowed to sleep upon. Just like floating on a cloud, it was.

Then he pictured in his mind's eye the old loghouse: the bare pine floors, the patchwork quilts, the prickly cornhusk mattress. The oil lamps and the candles and the scrubbed board table. The water buckets underneath the washbench.

Just then Emily glanced down to see why he was so quiet. Straightaway she noticed the furrow on his brow. "What's the matter, hinny? Have thee a headpain?"

"No, Mama, I'm fine," he answered. "But, Mama . . . " He knew he shouldn't ask, but he just had to know. "Are we poor folk?"

"Poor folk!" His mother's voice rose in astonishment. "Poor folk!" she repeated. "Why, Willie, how could you ask such a question when we have so much? A stout loghouse thy grandpa built those many years ago. And a strong papa who's willing to labour both day and night for his family. A fine forest we have back of the house chockful of winter fuel. Our own spring just a hop, skip, and a jump down the hill, pouring forth pure water both winter and summer. And food we always have . . . though sometimes it be only turnips."

At the mention of turnips Willie wrinkled his nose and made his mother laugh. Then she turned her face away and gazed out the window. When she turned back again he noticed that her eyes had gone all soft and misty. "And so much love we have, Willie. Now then, how could we be poor folk with all these many blessings?"

Willie sat quiet and thought for a moment, then he looked up so their eyes met. And a wonderful smile passed between them.

"Thank you, Mama," he said.

Bernice Thurman Hunter was a storyteller from an early age, but it was not until her children were grown that she began to get her work published. Now she is one of Canada's favourite authors of historical fiction, with a dozen books to her credit, including the Booky trilogy, *Hawk and Stretch*, the Margaret books, *Amy's Promise* (winner of the Red Cedar Award), *Janey's Choice*, *The Firefighter*, and *The Railroader*.

One of Bernice's greatest strengths as a writer is the ability to bring the past to vivid life for her readers. She draws many of her characters and situations from real life. Lamplighter paints an authentic picture of life in Northern Ontario in the 1880s, at the time her own father was growing up.